SAM AND THE KILLER ROBOT

JUDITH ROSSELL

LITTLE HARE
www.littleharebooks.com

Little Hare Books
8/21 Mary Street, Surry Hills
NSW 2010 AUSTRALIA

www.littleharebooks.com

Text copyright © Judith Rossell 2007
Illustrations copyright © Judith Rossell 2007
Cover illustrations © Judith Rossell 2007

First published in 2007

National Library of Australia
Cataloguing-in-Publication entry
Rossell, Judith.
Sam and the killer robot.

For primary school children.
ISBN 978 1 921272 10 3 (pbk.).

1. Robots - Juvenile fiction. 2. Insects - Juvenile
fiction. 3. Human-alien encounters - Juvenile fiction.
I. Title.

A823.4

Cover design by Serious Business
Set in 11.5/16.5pt Bookman by Clinton Ellicott
Printed in China by Imago

5 4 3 2 1

For Christopher, Rebecca, their mother
and their grandmother

Chapter One

For days there had been news reports on TV about the strange lights appearing in the sky. Some people said they were flying saucers, filled with aliens who were coming to invade the earth or to steal people away and do weird alien experiments to them. TV experts said the mysterious lights were meteors, or blobs of gas in the stratosphere, or birds, or planes.

Sam Miller ached to see a mysterious light. He longed desperately to see a flying saucer, and he wouldn't even have minded having weird alien experiments done to him. He would have welcomed them. His friend from school, Max, said he'd seen a light from his bedroom window. Sam didn't know whether to believe him or not: Max was always making things up. Sam had stared up into the sky until his eyes watered, but it had always stayed completely empty of anything interesting.

Until the first day of the school holidays.

Sam was on his way to Magic Mart to buy milk. He was feeling happy, with two fat, empty weeks stretching out in front of him. No school. Sam felt his mouth smiling all by itself. He stuck out his arms like the wings of a plane and spun around. Moriarty, running beside him like some kind of floppy grey rug, started to bark loudly.

Sam tilted his head back and looked up at the sky, still spinning. Bluish, greyish, little patches of clear. Nothing of interest. *No school, no school, no school,* sang in Sam's head.

Suddenly, out of nowhere, a brilliant orange light flashed across one of the clear patches of sky and disappeared behind a cloud. Sam stopped spinning, stumbled, and fell over. *What?* The orange light had been so bright the streak was still there in his eyes and he saw it everywhere, like after a camera flash, but now the sky seemed empty again and just as usual. For a second or two, Sam lay on his back on the footpath and stared up into the peaceful sky. *Was that really . . .?*

Moriarty was whining worriedly, licking and pawing at him. Sam took a breath, sat up and then got to his feet, still staring up at the sky. Blindly, he patted Moriarty's anxious head.

'Not to worry, dog,' he said, the flash of orange

light still at the back of his eyes, but fading now. For a few more moments he stood and gazed up into the empty sky, feeling the happiness bubble up inside him. *He'd seen one. He'd finally seen one.* He couldn't wait to tell Max.

'Come on then, dog,' he said at last.

The rest of the way up to Magic Mart, Sam hardly looked where he was going. But although he scanned the sky from side to side, he didn't see anything else up there, except for the clouds and a couple of high-flying seagulls.

Sam's family always did their shopping at Magic Mart because Uncle Andy was the manager. Sam's elder sister, Em, always moaned about Magic Mart, saying it was dirty and disorganised, but Sam liked it. Magic Mart was a tall brick building standing by itself up on the cliff, beyond the pier at the end of the foreshore. According to Dad, it had once been a cinema and before that a ship's chandler, whatever that was. Now it was a supermarket.

Sam tied Moriarty's lead to a pole at the front of the shop, gave him a comforting pat on the head, took one more look up at the empty sky and went inside.

Magic Mart was always darkish and a bit grimy.

Boxes were piled up everywhere. Sam could hear voices, some kind of wailing music and the *ahhh-ahhh* noise of the refrigeration. There were beach balls and buckets and spades hanging from the roof. Piles of weird-looking dried salted fish. Tinned food with labels in different languages, so you had to guess what was inside by the picture. Dog collars, clothes-pegs, hard black loaves of bread. All kinds of things.

'Milk, milk, milk,' Sam sang to himself. What kind of milk did aliens drink, he wondered. Green alien milk from alien cows with three heads, probably. He threaded his way past a teetering pile of boxes of coloured ice-cream cones to reach the cool room, his favourite part of Magic Mart. Stepping inside was like stepping into winter. There was a swirling, icy wind, a shuddering noise and a strange chemical smell. If he stayed long enough, patches of blue would appear on the backs of his hands and his ears and nose would go numb. It was excellent.

The milk shelves in the cool room were filled with rows of smart-looking purple bottles labelled, encouragingly, MØLK. Sam picked up one bottle and discovered that MØLK was a Scandinavian health drink made of yeast extract and fish oil and other healthy things. He hesitated. Maybe Mum would enjoy healthy MØLK in her coffee for a change. But she had said normal milk like she really meant it. Not MØLK, then. At the end of the rows of bottles there was a cluster of other things jumbled together. A cheese-flavoured tofu drink. Some big bottles of banana custard. And . . . Sam pounced on a white carton. Long-Life Cow Milk, it said on the label. Excellent.

On his way back down the aisle towards the checkout, Sam bumped unexpectedly into Uncle Andy. He had appeared suddenly around the end of an aisle, carrying an enormous pile of boxes and, *bash*, Sam walked straight into him. The boxes scattered, skidding across the floor. Uncle Andy did some awkward juggling, trying to keep hold of the last of the pile. He looked like an animated spider, all arms and legs and elbows. Sam helped pick up the boxes and, although he tried not to, he couldn't stop giggling.

'Sorry, Uncle Andy,' he snorted. 'Umm . . . hello.'

Uncle Andy paused, chewing something. He swallowed. 'Hello,' he said.

Sam looked up and sighed. Uncle Andy had been acting strangely for weeks. A few days ago, for example, Sam had found him in his office covered with dust and little bits of gravel. Normally he was an enthusiastic kind of adult, full of schemes and plans, always waving his bony arms around. But recently he'd been looking oddly blank. His voice seemed different, too. Sort of flat and even. Mechanical.

'Are you okay?' asked Sam, piling the scattered boxes into a neat stack.

There was a pause. Uncle Andy seemed to be thinking. Then he said, 'Okay,' in the same flat voice.

'Really? Oh. Good,' said Sam with a doubtful laugh. 'That's good. Well, I'd best be going, I suppose.' He picked up his carton of Long-Life Cow Milk from where it had fallen—luckily it hadn't broken—and turned to go. But just then he had his first proper look at the pile of boxes and he stopped dead in amazement.

On every box was a picture of the most incredible robot. It was silver with swirling red eyes and clutching claws for hands. In the picture, it looked like the robot was zooming along on its tank-like wheels, shooting bolts of red light from its dazzling eyes.

Feeling dazed, Sam grabbed the top box from the pile. There was writing all around the robot in different languages. The only English bit Sam could find was one line. It said: 'Build You Own Killer Robot Now Today'.

'Wow,' breathed Sam. He turned the box over. On the front there was a picture of a very happy lady, just about to take a bite from what looked like a flat, square, green biscuit. There was some squiggly foreign writing across the top, and underneath it said: 'Bisky Bricks. Blocks of Munching Delight. Delicious and Good for All Peoples. Contains Kelp'.

Sam turned the box back over and looked again at the amazing robot. This time he saw another bit of English in a little circle: 'Part Inside. Collect All Parts'. Underneath there was a tiny drawing. Sam recognised one of the robot's clutching-claw hands.

'Wow,' he said again, glancing up at Uncle Andy. 'This looks like an amazing model.'

After a pause Uncle Andy said, 'Amazing model.'

This time Sam didn't notice Uncle Andy's strange new voice: he was too busy looking at the price of the boxes of Bisky Bricks and counting his money. There was change from the milk money, and he'd just got some pocket money from Dad as well. Sam counted on his fingers to see how many boxes he could get. Three. Quickly he searched through the pile. On each box, under where it said 'Part Inside. Collect All Parts', there was a different drawing. Sam found one that looked like a robot arm and one that looked like a shoulder. He grabbed all three boxes and picked up the Long-Life Cow Milk again. He couldn't wait to get home to start work on the robot. How many boxes of Bisky Bricks would he need to get all the parts?

For a second Sam thought he heard a faint, buzzing, scrabbling sound from inside one of the boxes. As if something was alive in there. As if something was trying to get out. He shook the box, and held it up to his ear, but no, there was nothing.

He shrugged. He must have been mistaken.

Outside, someone called out, 'Hey, Sam. Hey, Moriarty.'

Sam turned around. 'Hey, Max,' he said.

Max was climbing out of his mum's car, which was parked beside the road. He jogged over. 'Mum's shopping. What's going on?' He patted Moriarty on the head. 'Hey, what've you got there?'

Sam showed him the robot picture on the Bisky Bricks box. 'Isn't it amazing? I'm going to build it. There's one piece in each box. I've got a hand and an arm and a shoulder, they should join together, I think. And, hey, Max. Guess what I saw . . .'

'Wow,' gasped Max, grabbing the box. 'This looks so excellent. Look at its eyes. "Build You Own Killer Robot Now Today." Wow, Sam. Hey, I'll make one too. We'll have one each. We can make them fight. Did you get them in here? I'm getting some straight away.' He handed the box back to Sam and rushed into Magic Mart.

Max was always like that, charging around like a whirlwind. Sam called, 'See you,' after him, but Max had already gone.

'Come on, dog,' he said to Moriarty.

Chapter Two

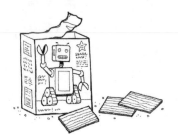

Hurrying in through the front gate of his house, Sam was still gazing at the picture of the robot on the back of the Bisky Bricks box, so he didn't notice that his little sister Steph was digging a trench in the front garden. At least he didn't notice until he caught his foot in it and fell full length with a thump into the geraniums.

'What the . . .?' he spluttered, his mouth full of leaves and dirt.

'Watch where you're going,' Steph snapped. 'Nice one, Sam.'

'What are you doing? Trying to kill me?' Sam shoved the anxious, licking Moriarty away, got back to his feet and collected his shopping. 'It's really stupid to dig holes in the front path, Steph.'

'You should look where you're going,' she said grumpily, using her spade to smooth out the pile of earth she'd dug. 'You've made a real mess. Thanks, Sam.'

Sam made an aggravated noise in his throat but didn't stop to argue. He had a robot to build.

His older sister, Em, was sitting at the kitchen table eating toast, drinking orange juice and admiring a length of sparkly pink fabric. As Sam walked in she was singing, toastily, the song for her dancing concert.

'*Sparkle, sparkle, like a star,*
Sweet as sugar, sweet as pie,
Sparkling just as if we are
Like the stars up in the sky.'

Even though Sam had heard this horrible song many, many times, it still made him feel really sick. He was dreading Em's dancing concert. Maybe he'd get a terrible disease, and then he wouldn't have to go. Moriarty, however, liked singing. He bounded across to Em and started to howl enthusiastically, wagging his tail.

Em stopped singing with a frown. 'Hello there,' she said crossly.

'Guess what?' Sam dumped his shopping onto the table and helped himself to a piece of toast. He broke it in two and gave half to Moriarty, who snapped it up like a crocodile.

'You shouldn't feed him at the table,' said Em.

'And you should teach him manners. Other dogs learn tricks. Not this idiot dog, though.'

'He's good at other things,' Sam said defensively. 'Anyway, guess what?'

Em snorted. 'Yeah, right. Eating.' She stomped out of the kitchen, trailing sparkly pink fabric behind her like a cape.

It was true that Moriarty wasn't good at learning things. Sam had tried to teach him to shake hands but Moriarty had never really understood what was needed. However, Em was right: he was an excellent eater. He ate all kinds of things. Once he ate a dozen raw eggs, shells, carton and all. He ate green tomatoes off the bushes in the garden and apples off the apple tree. At the beach, he ate dead fish and seaweed and slimy things washed up by the tide. Moriarty would have liked to eat Patrick's cat food as well, but Mum fed Patrick up on top of the fridge. Moriarty would sit looking up hopefully and drooling so much there would be a puddle.

'Silly great lump.' Mum came into the kitchen with Sam's baby sister, Molly, on her hip, and pushed Moriarty out of the way so she could get the coffee pot. 'Sam, please move this foolish dog. Did you get the milk? Oh, good.' She planted Molly into her high chair and handed her a piece of toast. Molly took the toast in her fat starfish hands and started to crumple it to bits. Mum picked up the Long-Life Cow Milk, opened the carton, sniffed it suspiciously and then added some to her coffee.

'Guess what?' said Sam, opening the boxes of Bisky Bricks and pouring the contents out onto the table. 'I saw one of those UFO things. In the sky. It was like this . . .' He zipped his hand through the air to show how fast the orange light had flown through the sky. 'It was amazing.'

'Really? Goodness. Well, Sam, that's . . . oh, Molly don't do that . . .'

Molly was getting big enough to reach out from her high chair and grab things from the kitchen bench. Mum rescued the Long-Life Cow Milk carton from Molly's grasp and seized a cloth to mop up the mess. Molly started to scream. She hated having things taken away from her.

While Mum wiped and comforted Molly, Sam described the orange light in detail and searched through the Bisky Bricks for the robot parts. The Bisky Bricks were a dark brownish-green colour. They looked like bits of corrugated cardboard, about the same size as playing cards. Sam sniffed one. It smelled like compost, or like seaweed drying in the sun. He took a bite. It was chewy and claggy and tasted faintly fishy. He gave the rest of it to Moriarty, who chomped and gulped, his eyes bulging.

'What's this?' Mum jiggled Molly on her hip and nibbled the corner of a Bisky Brick. She made a face and fed the rest of it into Moriarty's waiting mouth. She picked up one of the boxes, looked at the happy lady eating on the front and then at the amazing robot on the back. '"Build You Own Killer Robot Now Today",' she read out. 'Are you building you own killer robot now today, Sam?'

'Mmm,' said Sam. 'Well, maybe not now today. I need lots more parts. Everyone'll have to eat these things all holidays so I can get them all.'

'Well . . .' said Mum.

The robot parts were small, compact and neat looking. They felt heavier than Sam had expected. They were silver, with a smooth, flat sheen. Sam's fingers itched to try to fit them together.

'What's going on?' Em marched into the kitchen lugging the sewing machine. 'Mum, you said you'd help me with this costume.'

'I did. I will,' said Mum.

Em plonked the sewing machine onto the table, picked up a Bisky Brick and took a bite. 'Yuck. What is this? It's like, *euuggh*, fish. Like fishy grass.'

'"Contains Kelp",' Mum read from the label.

'What's kelp?' asked Em with her mouth full.

'Seaweed,' said Mum.

'*Eeyeww.*' Em tried to spit out the bits. '*Bleh,*

bleh, gross. I'm not eating seaweed. Trust you, Sam, to get something stupid and disgusting. I told you not to go to Magic Mart. That Uncle Andy ...'

'He was very strange this morning,' said Sam. 'Even stranger than normal. Can you see any instructions anywhere?' He peered inside one of the boxes.

'Instructions for what? For how to be sick? Step one: eat a disgusting seaweed-flavoured thing bought by your idiot baby brother. Step two: vomit like a huge fountain.'

'Ha ha.' Sam ripped one of the empty boxes apart but there were no instructions anywhere. 'I'll just have to go by the picture.' He grabbed the scissors from the table and started to cut the back off the box.

'Not with the sewing scissors, Sam,' said Mum.

'No, no, okay,' said Sam, cutting quickly. 'There. Done.'

He collected up the three robot parts, the picture of the robot and a handful of Bisky Bricks. 'Come on, then,' he said to Moriarty. 'Let's get started.'

Mum's voice followed him down the passage-way, calling out something, but Sam didn't really hear it properly.

In his bedroom, his mouth full of claggy Bisky Brick, Sam emptied the contents of a desk drawer onto the floor. Pens and pencils and bits and pieces scattered everywhere. He prised a half-used tube of model glue from where it was stuck at the back of the drawer and put it ready on the desk. He swept a whole stack of clothes and books and bits of homework from the desk onto the floor, sat down and laid the three robot parts out in a row. They gleamed in the light from the window. He stared at the robot picture he'd taped to the wall. He picked up the piece that was obviously one of the robot hands, and the longish piece that he thought was an arm, then tried to fit them together.

From the bed, Moriarty gave a low growl. Sam swivelled around. Normally, when Sam was working at the desk, Moriarty was curled up on the bed, grunting and snorting and occasionally making horrible smells. Now he was staring fixedly across at Sam with the hairs on his neck standing up.

'What's up with you?' asked Sam. 'Bad dream?'

He swivelled back and picked up the third robot part. The shoulder. He turned the parts this way, that way, trying to see how they might fit together.

Suddenly Moriarty growled again, a bit louder. Like he really meant it. Sam felt the back of his neck prickle. Before he could turn around again, the robot parts seemed to move in his hands. One piece turned right over. There was a smooth *click, click, click* and the three pieces connected themselves neatly together.

'Wow,' breathed Sam. This really was an incredible model. He must have lined the parts up the correct way at last, and maybe there were magnets inside the pieces that made them join up to each other. In his hands was a robot arm about as long as a pencil: shoulder, arm and clutching-claw hand. The three parts had connected so well and so neatly that Sam couldn't see where they joined. He couldn't pull them apart again. He flexed the silver arm. The joints moved smoothly and cleanly. The clutching claw opened and shut with a snapping noise.

'Look at this,' he said, turning to show the arm to Moriarty.

Snap, snap, went the clutching claw. Moriarty growled, deep down in his chest.

'Don't be frightened,' said Sam, holding the arm out so Moriarty could see it was safe. 'It's just a model, it's only . . .'

The arm gave a sudden twist in his hand, snapping its claw viciously. Sam gasped, jumped, and dropped it onto the floor. *Snap, snap, snap.* It scooted across the floor and shot under the bed. There was a scuttling noise, another *snap*, and then silence. Sam and Moriarty stared at each other. If it was possible for a dog to have an expression that said, 'I tried to warn you', Moriarty had that expression now.

Sam got down on his hands and knees and peered underneath the bed. It was dark, and there were lots of things under there, socks, old toys and forgotten things. He thought he saw something gleam at the back in the shadows. He picked up his cricket bat from beside the desk, reached it cautiously under the bed and gave the gleaming thing a poke.

Snap! Sam felt the bat jerk in his hand. He brought it out and saw a little bit was missing from the end, in the shape of a clutching claw. He avoided Moriarty's accusing stare.

'Well, it's an amazing model,' Sam said, carefully getting to his feet and stepping away from the bed. 'Normally things that come free like this are plastic and pretty pathetic. This is a top-quality model.'

He sucked in a breath through his teeth and added, 'I just have to catch it. That's all.'

Chapter Three

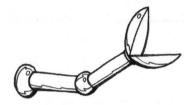

Sam bent down and looked under the bed again. He couldn't see the robot arm but he could sense it under there, waiting.

'Okay, then,' he said to Moriarty. 'It'll be easy enough to catch it. I just need something longish, and tough. Wait here.'

But Moriarty leaped off the bed and shot out of the bedroom.

'Chicken,' said Sam.

He shut the bedroom door behind them. If the arm got loose in the house he might never get it back. Outside in the garden shed, while Moriarty sniffed and sneezed in the cobwebby corners, Sam found what he wanted. The long metal rake with the tough-looking metal handle. The big torch. A huge pair of leather gardening gloves. He also found an empty paint can. It seemed pretty strong, although it was rusty in patches, and it had a good, tight-fitting lid.

Carrying the rake, the gloves, the can and the torch, Sam headed back inside to his bedroom. Moriarty sidled reluctantly into the room and jumped onto the bed looking nervous. Sam shone the torch under the bed. He could see the gleaming robot arm lurking behind a shoe. As he watched, the clutching claw seemed to rear up as if getting ready to attack. Probably it just seemed that way in the wavering torchlight, Sam told himself firmly. He swallowed.

He laid the torch down on the floor so it shone on the silver arm, pulled the gloves firmly onto his hands and grabbed the rake. Gingerly, he fished under the bed.

Snap, snap. The clutching claw grabbed at the metal prongs of the rake and hung on. There was an angry, scrabbling noise. Sam dragged the rake out from under the bed. The robot arm came too, twisting and snapping. Just before it reached the open floor it let go of the rake and scrambled back under the bed.

Sam grabbed the torch and flashed it around under the bed. There it was, behind an old knitted teddy. He could see the silver gleam. He fished again with the rake, more determinedly, bringing the rake prongs down behind the arm and dragging it out. It fought all the way, but this time Sam was ready. Holding the struggling robot arm firmly in place with the rake, he reached down with one hand and grabbed it as hard as he could, just behind the clutching claw. Like he'd seen snake handlers do on TV. He let go of the rake. The robot arm twisted and writhed in his gloved hand, the claw snapping from side to side.

Moriarty started to bark.

'Shut up,' shouted Sam.

Moriarty barked even louder.

With his free hand, Sam grabbed the paint can and lowered the snapping robot arm into it. He let go as quickly as he could and banged the lid down on top. But the clutching claw was quicker. It grabbed hold of the tip of one of the glove fingers. Sam shrieked. The robot arm was half out of the can, snapping and scrabbling.

'*Arrghhh!*' Sam yelled. He desperately twisted his hand out of the huge glove. The glove fell into the can and the robot arm fell with it. Sam slammed the lid down. He felt the can shake. The arm rattled and snapped inside.

Sam grabbed the heavy torch and hammered the lid down tightly. That should keep it safe. He flopped down onto the bed with a big sigh of relief.

'You can stop that barking,' he said to Moriarty. 'You're all right now. It can't get out.'

They both looked at the can in the middle of the

floor. There was a small scrabbling sound, a *snap*, and then an ominous silence.

Sam's family usually ate lunch together on Saturdays, if Dad got home from work at Fridge World in time.

'Who's been digging holes in the front path?' he yelled as he stumbled into the kitchen, brushing bits of geranium leaves and dirt out of his hair. He gave Mum a smacking kiss on the side of her head, tripped over Moriarty—who immediately started barking in a panicky kind of way—waved at Sam and Em, pointed an accusing finger at Steph, made a cooing noise at Molly and plonked himself down at the table.

'Shut up, you foolish dog,' he said to Moriarty, giving him a pat.

Moriarty barked even louder and looked lovingly up into his face. After Sam, Dad was Moriarty's favourite person.

'What a morning. Seven fridges. Out the door. Two Freezomatic 5000s. Top of the range,' said Dad, helping himself to mashed potatoes, peas and sausages. 'Four new Icemasters. Excellent model, with the triple evaporator system. And a Chilltastic RV,' he nodded at the shiny new fridge in the corner. 'Like ours. I'm as hungry as a . . . I don't know,' he winked at Steph. 'What has a big appetite?'

'Well,' said Steph, seriously, 'an earthworm eats its own weight in dirt every single day. And some spiders can eat twice their weight in insects. Imagine that.' She waved her hands in the air, making the shape of an enormous pile of insects.

'Mmm,' said Dad. 'That's the kind of thing. Then I'm as hungry as a spider. But Steph—' he pointed his fork at her, 'no more holes in the front path. It's dangerous. Okay?'

Steph sighed gustily. 'Okay. Okay. I really should dig small trenches everywhere, though. Before I start excavating—'

'Excavating?' interrupted Mum. 'No. No excavating, Steph. Not in the front garden, anyway. You can dig up the back garden, if you must.'

Dad nodded. 'Back garden only,' he said with his mouth full. 'We don't want everyone falling into holes.'

Steph shrugged. Watching her moodily squashing peas with her fork, Sam thought this might be a good moment to change the subject.

'Guess what, Dad?' he said, quickly swallowing a claggy mouthful of Bisky Brick. 'I saw one of those lights in the sky today. It was amazing. Really bright orange, like they said on TV.'

Em made a scornful, disbelieving snorting

noise, but Dad said, 'Really, Sam? Good for you. Whereabouts?'

'On the foreshore. Going to Magic Mart. Oh, and, Dad, Uncle Andy was so weird this morning.'

Dad rolled his eyes. 'That'd be right,' he said. 'He's just like that terrible, unreliable SuperFrost fridge they brought out in the eighties. It looked okay from the outside, but inside it was a joke. Just a joke. That's my brother. Did I ever tell you about the time he tried to fly off our roof?'

'Yes,' said Sam and Em and Steph together.

Dad ignored this and carried on. 'With a parachute he made out of our mum's—your nan's—old knickers? I mean, they were really huge, sure, but all the same. A broken ankle, he got, and your nan was so angry.'

Uncle Andy was Dad's little brother, five years younger, and as far as Dad was concerned, Uncle Andy was still a badly behaved twelve-year-old.

Thinking about Uncle Andy reminded Sam of how many Bisky Bricks he needed to eat. It would be so much easier if someone else would help, and Dad was his last hope. Apart from Moriarty, nobody else in the family would eat any. Even Patrick, the cat, had refused to eat his food when Sam sprinkled broken-up Bisky Brick over the top. He had hissed angrily and shot outside like an offended ginger missile.

But Dad liked to eat all kinds of weird things. He liked that cheese with bits of blue mould inside it. He ate sausages spicy enough to make his eyes water. He sometimes drank whisky, which smelled to Sam like some kind of solvent. Surely he could be relied on to eat a box or two of Bisky Bricks.

Sam pushed the plate invitingly towards Dad, took a Bisky Brick off the top of the pile and bit into it. 'Mmm-mmm,' he said, chewing doggedly. 'Come on, Dad. Try one of these. They're delicious.'

Em and Steph both made noises like they were being sick and even Mum screwed up her nose.

'What's this?' asked Dad, helping himself to one, sniffing it suspiciously and taking his first experimental bite. He chewed, frowned, and chewed a bit more, looking determined.

Sam nodded, smiled encouragingly and nudged the plate of Bisky Bricks closer.

But all at once Dad gave up. He spat out a shower of chewed up Bisky Brick. 'Euggh!' He took a big gulp of water from his glass. 'No. I'm sorry, Sam, but that was about the worst thing I've ever tasted.' He ran his tongue around the inside of his mouth and shuddered.

Sam sighed as he picked bits of chewed up Bisky Brick out of his hair. At least he still had Moriarty. The rest of the family were going to be no help at all.

After lunch Sam went to his room, cautiously levered the lid off the paint tin and peered inside. The robot arm was lying quietly at the bottom, apparently lifeless. The leather gardening glove was in there too, but it was ripped into several ragged pieces. Sam jiggled the tin. Suddenly the arm came to life, writhing viciously. *Snap, snap, snap.* Sam jumped. He slammed the lid back on, banged it firmly in place and put the tin safely on the floor of his cupboard among the shoes. He shut the cupboard door carefully.

He looked at Moriarty, who looked back uneasily.

'All the same,' said Sam, 'It's going to be a really amazing robot. I can't wait to get the next bit.'

Chapter Four

In the kitchen, Em was driving the sewing machine like a racing car—*vroom, vroom*—pink sparkly fabric flashing. Dad was washing up. Mum was feeding Molly something mushy and writing a list. Steph was looking through a magnifying glass at some dirt in an ice-cream container and drawing things in a notebook.

'Can I go and get some more Bisky Bricks from Magic Mart?' asked Sam.

'What?' said Mum, looking up from her list. 'Why? You haven't finished them already?'

'Nearly,' said Sam. It was sort of true. He'd started on the second box.

'Get something nicer,' said Em, taking her foot off the accelerator for a second. 'They're really disgusting.'

Dad made an agreeing noise.

'I want to get all the parts for the robot,' said Sam, staring at Em's sparkly fabric. For a moment he was dazzled and forgot what he was saying. Then he shook his head and went on. 'It's amazing. I don't mind eating all the Bisky Bricks. I'll eat just them. All holidays. I don't mind.'

'*Euughh*,' said Em, pulling a face. 'Gross.'

'I don't want you eating only those,' said Mum. 'There is such a thing as a balanced diet. We don't even know what's in them.'

Sam sighed. Sometimes parents seemed to just make difficulties. 'They're good for you,' he said. '"Delicious and Good for All Peoples", it says on the box. They've got kelp in them.'

'I suppose you can get a couple more boxes,' said Mum, 'and see how you go. I want you eating proper meals, though. I don't want you just eating kelp all the time. That can't be healthy. You're not a . . . Steph, what eats kelp?'

'Fish. Sea urchins. Snails. Crabs,' said Steph without looking up from her dirt.

'You're not a crab, Sam,' said Mum, wagging a finger, pretending this was an important piece of advice. 'Always remember that.' She rummaged in her handbag for money.

Sam and Steph both sniggered. Molly laughed as well and banged her spoon on the high chair, spattering mushy blobs all over the table. Em squealed and pulled her sparkly pink sewing away from the bits of baby food.

'Thanks, Mum,' said Sam, taking the money.

Moriarty had been watching anxiously, hoping for something to happen, and when he saw Sam reach for the dog lead behind the kitchen door he gave a delighted whining bark, wagging his whole shaggy body. Sam clipped the lead onto his collar.

'Come on, then, dog,' he said.

All the way along the foreshore, Sam gazed upwards hoping to see another mysterious orange light. He didn't see anything in the sky, but standing on the pier was a strange-looking man dressed in a dark suit. He had a bushy black beard that covered most of his face. At first Sam thought he also had a strange bushy hairstyle, but when he got a bit closer he saw the man was wearing a black furry hat. How odd. He was also wearing black leather gloves and was holding a small, shiny black suitcase. The man looked out of place on the wooden pier, with the seagulls flying around him and a couple of men fishing from deckchairs nearby. The strange man was shading his eyes and looking about. Up at the sky, and then across to the cliff below Magic Mart, which was pitted with the shadowy entrances to caves.

Sam watched the man for a moment or two but nothing happened, so he shrugged and climbed up the road to Magic Mart.

The Bisky Brick boxes were piled in an enormous pyramid just inside the front entrance of the shop. Row after row of killer robots, zooming along on their tank-like wheels, red eyes swirling. There was no sign of Uncle Andy.

Mum had said to get a couple of boxes—which meant two, of course. If only Sam had more money saved up, but he always spent his pocket money straight away. Sam and Em were both spenders. Steph was the only saver in the family. She had a hoard of money locked in a metal tin hidden in her bedroom.

Sam looked at the money Mum had given him. He counted on his fingers and worked out that he could get four boxes. Four wasn't much more than two, after all.

He picked up the boxes one by one, and looked carefully at the little drawing of the robot part. He lined up several boxes on a shelf so he could compare them. Finally he chose four which contained parts that looked like they might fit together. He was clutching the boxes and gazing at the impressive pyramid when someone ran breathlessly into the shop. Sam looked around. It was Max. Sam grinned. But Max hardly looked at him: he just ran to the pile of boxes and started to grab one after another until he had an armful of eight or nine.

'Hi, Max,' said Sam.

Max glanced at him. 'What?' he said. Sam noticed that Max had bits of Bisky Brick stuck in the braces on his teeth.

'I just said hi . . .'

'Oh. Hi, Sam,' said Max. 'Sorry. Mum and Dad don't know I've come out. I had to sneak out and I've got to be quick.'

'How are you going with the robot?' asked Sam.

Max looked over his shoulder and then said rapidly, 'I got three parts this morning. One of those legs.' He pointed at the picture of the tank-like wheels. 'It went zooming off straight away. It crashed through the wall. It made this hole in the wall. It was so great. It was amazing.' He swallowed and went on. 'Dad says I can't make any more. He says it's too dangerous. I should stick to Lego, he says.' Max rolled his eyes. 'I've locked the leg thing up in Dad's toolbox. It's really strong: you can hear it bashing around in there.'

Max grabbed a couple more boxes and rushed off, clutching the pile awkwardly.

'Bye, then,' Sam called after him. He followed Max to the checkout, walking more slowly. He thought maybe he'd keep the robot away from Mum and Dad, just for the moment. They might misunderstand it. Maybe they wouldn't let him keep it. That would be terrible.

Back home, he rushed inside and emptied the boxes of Bisky Bricks onto the kitchen table. Moriarty was whining nervously but Sam didn't pay any attention. He rummaged through the scattered pile for the robot pieces, chewing on a Bisky Brick that had found its way into his mouth. He didn't listen to Em shouting at him for covering her sparkly pink fabric with stupid seaweed snacks and asking why had he bought them anyway, and saying no way was she going to eat any of them and he needn't expect it. Sam found the four new robot pieces, and grabbing yet another handful of Bisky Bricks to chew on— he was starting to get quite used to the taste—he hurried along to his room. He shut the door and carefully laid the four new robot pieces in a line on his desk.

As before, the model pieces were surprisingly heavy and smoothly silver and gleaming. On the bed, Moriarty gave a low warning growl and in the bottom of the cupboard, there came a muffled snapping and rattling from the paint tin. Sam took no notice. His hands were running over the pieces of the robot, feeling the smooth, heavy shapes. Three of them were squarish. One was longish. Sam picked the pieces up and turned them this way and that. Then, just like before, there was a smooth *click, click, click*, and the four pieces moved in his hands and fitted themselves together. Three pieces joined neatly to form the robot's head, and the longish piece made the neck. Sam held the little model head in his hands, turning it from side to side. He felt it quiver faintly and there was a low humming noise like a distant engine.

Suddenly, *blink, blink*. Two little red lights came on. Sam jumped, dropping the head onto the desktop. It lay there, staring up at him with glowing red eyes. Sam gazed back at it. He felt like he couldn't look away. The robot eyes seemed to be staring right inside his head, into his brain. He couldn't even blink. The staring eyes seemed to grow larger, and the rest of the room became darker and blurred and unimportant.

Moriarty growled again, more loudly, but Sam hardly heard him. He was being drawn towards two enormous red lights. Like the headlights of a train, he thought. And there was a message for him. The lights had something important to tell him. Closer and closer they came: they seemed to surround him. The whole world was made up of red light . . .

Suddenly, *crash*, he was knocked off his chair, and Moriarty was licking his face and whining anxiously. Sam gasped, feeling disorientated, as if he had been woken abruptly from a deep sleep. He lay on the floor, drained and exhausted. He reached up a shaky hand and patted Moriarty's head.

'Wow,' he breathed at last. He sat up, untangled himself from the fallen chair and the worried dog, and got to his feet. 'That was amazing. It's got something like hypnotism in it. It must be some kind of computer.'

He picked up an old school T-shirt from the floor and—taking care not to look directly into the eyes—quickly wrapped the robot head in the shirt, around and around, until the red eyes glowed only faintly through the fabric.

On the whole, Sam thought, it might be best to keep the robot's head and arm separate for the moment. The arm was still safe inside the paint tin. He poked the T-shirt-wrapped head to the back of his sock drawer, squashed socks around it and pushed the drawer firmly shut.

He took a deep breath of relief. 'Thanks, dog,' he said, offering Moriarty a Bisky Brick from the pile on the desk.

To Sam's surprise, Moriarty sniffed suspiciously at the Bisky Brick, whined, and turned away.

Sam shrugged. 'No? Well, I'm starting to quite like them,' he said, chewing. 'And, you know, I can't wait to get the rest of the pieces of this robot. I'll make a leg next, I think. It's going to be incredible when it's finished.'

Moriarty gave a huge gusty sigh and turned his head to the wall.

Chapter Five

When it was starting to get dark, Mum sent Sam and Moriarty outside to call Steph for dinner. Sam went over to where Steph was digging and looked down into the sandy trench. It was already quite deep and stretched for several metres along the back garden. There was a big pile of dirt and another big pile of rocks. She must have been working hard all afternoon.

'Hiya,' Sam said. 'Dinner's ready.'

Steph looked very dirty and tired, but happy. She stopped digging, grinned at Sam and reached up a filthy hand to pat Moriarty's head.

'Hi,' she said.

'What's this all about?' asked Sam. He peered down into the shadowy hole. 'What're you looking for?'

'Well, whatever's here,' said Steph. 'I'm doing a survey. It's very interesting. Did you know that in one square metre of soil, there are probably one thousand insects? Did you know that some worms go as deep as five metres underground? Also, I was hoping to find some cicada nymphs. You know, Sam, they spend maybe seventeen years underground, like grubs. Then they come up into the air and change completely, grow wings, fly around, and live for only three days. Isn't that amazing? Imagine if we lived like that? Imagine that.'

Steph looked as if she was imagining just that, and thinking it would be an excellent way to live. Sam thought briefly about it and decided that even spending seventeen years underground as a grub would not be as bad as sitting through Em's dancing concert.

'What've you found so far?' he asked.

'Heaps of things. Rocks. Worms. Beetles.' She waved her hands around. 'It's so interesting down here.' She picked up the spade again happily. 'You can help, if you like,' she added, as if granting Sam an enormous favour. 'I'm going to dig this trench along under the house and then start another one over there by that tree.'

'Err, well, thanks, Steph,' said Sam. 'But you know. Things to do. Anyway, dinner's ready. Mum says for you to come inside.'

Steph dug out one more spadeful of dirt and then reluctantly climbed out of the hole. She banged her hands together and said, 'I s'pose I'll have to wash . . .'

Sam grinned. Steph was very, very dirty. 'I guess so,' he said.

They turned to walk back to the house. Sam automatically glanced up. It was a clear evening and a few stars were already shining. He wasn't thinking of much, just wondering what was for dinner, when suddenly a dazzling orange light streaked across the dark sky. It was brilliant. Much brighter than before. Flying in a fast curving line. It disappeared behind the trees at the back fence. Moriarty started to bark loudly. Sam gasped, still staring up at the sky, and grabbed Steph by the arm.

'Did you see that?'

Steph was looking startled. 'I saw a sort of flash . . .' she said doubtfully.

'Oh, Steph, you missed it,' said Sam. 'It went right across. Like that.' He swept an arm across the sky, from behind the house over to the back fence and down towards the sea. When he blinked, he could see the trace of the light's path at the back of his eyes.

Steph looked disappointed. 'I was looking down at the ground,' she said. 'What was it, do you think? Some kind of giant firefly maybe.'

'I don't think so,' said Sam. 'I think it was an

alien spaceship. Oh, shut up, dog.' He patted Moriarty comfortingly. 'It's just a light. It can't hurt you all the way up there.'

At dinner Sam told everyone about the second mysterious light.

Mum said, 'Oh, really, Sam? That's nice,' and Dad said, 'Good for you, Sam.' But there were too many other things going on for them to really pay attention.

Mum kept sending Steph back to the bathroom because clumps of dirt were falling from her hair into her spaghetti. Em was describing her costume and the dance she would be doing at the concert. She kept getting up to demonstrate different steps. She also did an imitation of Bethany, a girl from her dancing class, who apparently danced with a foolish, simpering smile on her face and her bottom poking out. Molly yelled and tossed bits of food around. Moriarty kept shooting out from under the table, rushing to the back window and barking anxiously up at the sky.

Sam chewed up some more Bisky Bricks. He was feeling happy. He'd seen two mysterious lights, which was more than Max had. He had a robot arm and a robot head in his bedroom and soon he'd be getting more parts. The first day of his holidays had gone really well.

The next morning at breakfast time, while Moriarty slumbered underneath the kitchen table, Sam doggedly chewed his way through eight more Bisky Bricks—he was well into the third box— and tried to ignore the sound of all three of his sisters yelling. Sometimes Sam felt like he had altogether too many sisters.

Em and Steph were shouting about the fact that Steph had used some of Em's special body lotion and her toothbrush to clean rocks in the bathroom basin, and Molly was screaming in sympathy.

Sam was only half listening. The sunlight was glancing off his glass of orange juice, and the light was dazzling. It caught his eye and he found himself staring at it without blinking. He didn't seem to be able to look away.

Mum came into the room and passed between the juice glass and the window, casting a shadow. Sam jumped, blinked and looked up. He felt dazed.

'Stop all this bickering,' said Mum. She was wearing her dressing gown and carrying a list. She picked up Molly from the floor and grabbed the coffee pot with her other hand.

'But, Mum . . .' said Em and Steph together.

'No. Enough,' said Mum firmly. 'Your father is trying to sleep.'

Mum always wanted Dad to rest on the weekends. She thought he worked too hard during the week. But Dad usually only stayed in bed for a few extra hours, leafing through his collection of *Refrigeration Now* magazines, and then he would get up and go back in to work, even though he was meant to be having a day off. Dad loved work. 'Fridges won't sell themselves,' he said.

Mum poured herself some coffee and looked around for the milk. 'Steph, what are those rocks doing on the table?'

'Nothing.' Steph looked guilty. Mum had said she wasn't to bring any more rocks into the house. She already had so many rocks in her bedroom that sometimes the floorboards creaked.

'Outside, Steph.'

'But, Mum, they're very interesting,' said Steph. 'They're sedimentary.'

'I don't care. Take them outside. Now, Steph. Don't look like that. They're rocks, they're used to being outside. They prefer it.' While Steph gloomily collected up her rocks, Mum went on. 'So. How's that costume coming along, Em?'

'Okay, I guess,' said Em sulkily. 'There's a rehearsal this afternoon. Three o'clock.' She gulped some orange juice and added in an unconvincing off-hand tone, 'Ms Prance is going to announce the solo dancer today.'

There was a sudden silence. Sam and Steph met each other's gaze and rolled their eyes.

After a second, Mum cleared her throat and said, 'Do you know who . . .?'

Em shrugged.

'Well,' Steph, her arms full of rocks, took a breath and said belligerently, 'I bet that Bethany gets the part. Just like last time. And then you'll be yell, yell, yell all holidays . . .'

Em gave a shriek of rage. Sam sighed. If Steph wanted to pick a nasty fight with Em, this was the way to do it.

'Shut up,' shouted Mum, jiggling Molly who had started to yell again. 'Both of you. Steph, take those rocks outside. Right now. And don't make that kind of noise, it's very rude. Em, why don't you go and get the costume and we'll have a look at it.'

Sam watched Em and Steph stamp out of the room in opposite directions. He took another Bisky Brick and started chewing. Mum hushed Molly and sipped her coffee, looking at her list.

'Molly's party on Tuesday, Sam,' she said. 'Only two days to go.' And to Molly, she said, 'Your first birthday party, darling.'

Molly gurgled happily, waving her hands.

Because so many people had been seeing alien lights in the sky, Molly was going to have an outer-space alien birthday party. The invitations had pictures of little green Martians and rocket ships. All the guests were going to come dressed up as aliens. Sam already had a plan for his costume. He was going to cover his bike helmet with silver foil and make two antennae with wire and ping-pong balls.

Mum looked at her list. 'Sausage rolls. Party pies. Fairy bread. What else? Decorations. Sam, will you get some balloons and streamers at Magic Mart? And some more milk, please. And remind Uncle Andy about the party.'

'Sure,' said Sam. Uncle Andy was always excellent fun at parties. 'And I could get some more Bisky Bricks while I'm there. Maybe just a box or two. For the party.'

'No, Sam. No more. Not until you've eaten all the ones you got yesterday.' Mum sounded like she meant it. She nodded disapprovingly at the four full boxes of Bisky Bricks on the kitchen counter.

Although he had expected this, Sam sighed. 'Oh, go on, Mum,' he pleaded. 'It's an amazing model. I probably only need a few more parts.'

'No, Sam.' Mum sounded definite. Sam felt like arguing but at that moment Em pranced into the room wearing a half-finished sparkly pink dancing costume, and Mum immediately got up from the table and started fiddling and folding and pinning and talking to Em about hems and sequins.

Sam watched for a few moments as he swallowed a claggy, fishy mouthful of Bisky Brick. The trouble with Mum was that when she said no to something, she usually meant it. Dad was much easier to deal with. Maybe he'd have a word with Dad while Mum was busy with something else.

Now that even Moriarty was refusing to eat the Bisky Bricks, Sam really was on his own. Unless he got more money from somewhere it might be days before he got any more robot parts.

Chapter Six

Sam caught Dad at a good time, just as he was finishing his coffee and getting ready to leave for work. Sam leaned casually up against the bedroom door and said, 'Hey. Dad. So. What's new at Fridge World?'

Dad was enthusiastic. 'There's talk of a new model Cool King,' he said, rubbing his hands together.

Sam nodded. 'With the Multi-freeze ice feature.'

'Exactly right, Sam,' said Dad, slurping the last of his coffee. 'And the Icemasters are just walking out the door at the moment.'

'They've got that Double Evaporator System, haven't they?' said Sam.

'Triple,' corrected Dad. 'And the door-mounted ice dispenser. An excellent model.'

'They're not as good as the Chilltastic, though, are they?' asked Sam.

'But reliable,' said Dad, patting Moriarty on

the head. 'And good value.' He picked up his wallet and a handful of coins from the bedside table.

'Oh, by the way, Dad,' said Sam, cleverly choosing the perfect moment. 'I need to get a couple of things from Magic Mart. Could I get some pocket money in advance?'

'Here you go, then,' said Dad, handing over some coins. He was always happiest and most agreeable when he was talking about fridges.

Sam and Moriarty were just turning the corner onto the foreshore—Sam jingling his pocketful of money and Moriarty whining and wagging his tail and heaving enthusiastically on the lead— when Sam heard the sound of running footsteps together with a rattling noise.

'Sam! Sam! Wait for me!' It was Steph, running, panting, and clutching her money tin.

Sam stopped. 'Wait, dog,' he said.

Steph came running up. 'I want to go with you,' she gasped. 'I need some stuff.'

Mum and Dad said Steph couldn't go down to the shops by herself. She wasn't old enough. Sometimes she argued with them, and sometimes she went down the street by herself, but usually she went along with Em or Sam.

'Stuff?' said Sam, as they walked along the foreshore together. 'What stuff?'

'I want some containers for samples. And a new notebook,' said Steph. 'You know. Stuff like that.'

Sam thoughtfully eyed Steph's heavy-looking money tin. Dad had given him enough money for three more boxes of Bisky Bricks, but he'd need more than that to complete the robot. Maybe he could borrow some from Steph. It wasn't very likely: she was a determined saver and she never lent money, but maybe . . .

'Steph . . .' he started.

'Hey, Sam,' said Steph, not hearing him. 'Have you ever thought how weird it would be if we were mosquitoes?'

'What?' said Sam, confused by the abrupt change of subject.

'It would be so weird, wouldn't it?' said Steph. 'I mean, to start with we'd be living underwater and Mum and Dad would be flying around in the air. Mum would be sucking blood from people. Dad would be sucking the juice out of plants. Did you know it's only the lady mosquitoes who suck blood? But we'd never see them, because we'd be swimming around underwater. Wouldn't that be weird? Molly would probably still be a larva. And Em and you and me would be pupae. Imagine that.'

Steph looked out to sea, obviously imagining life as a mosquito pupa. Sam looked at his sister and thought, not for the first time, that sometimes she could be very strange.

'Steph . . .' he started again. 'Could you lend me some money?'

Steph clutched her money tin more tightly to her chest and looked suspiciously at him. 'No. Why?'

Even though he could tell it would be useless, Sam explained about the Bisky Bricks and the robot and how he needed just a few more parts. Before he had got halfway, Steph was shaking her head.

'No, I can't. I'm saving up. You get more pocket money than me, anyway. You should save up.'

'I'll pay you back,' said Sam.

'No. I need it,' said Steph. 'It's mine.'

Sam sighed, although he wasn't particularly disappointed. It had been worth a try, but he'd never managed to borrow money from Steph before. They walked on together in silence, Moriarty pulling on the lead, waving his tail and panting happily, Steph holding tightly to her money tin and darting glances at Sam as if she expected him to try to grab it.

As they climbed up the road at the end of the foreshore, Sam glimpsed the bearded stranger with the furry hat he'd seen on the pier the day before. It was only a brief glimpse as he walked briskly across the road in front of Magic Mart and disappeared inside, but Sam was sure it was the same man.

'See that man?' he said to Steph. But Steph wasn't interested in people. She was still thinking about life as a mosquito.

'You know, Sam, if we were mosquitoes, there'd be maybe two thousand of us kids in the family. Imagine that. A family with two thousand kids.'

Sam shrugged. There didn't seem to be anything to say about that. Having three sisters was bad enough. Two thousand sisters was something he didn't want to think about. He tied Moriarty's lead to the pole outside Magic Mart, patted him on the head and followed Steph inside.

There was still an enormous pyramid of Bisky Bricks boxes by the front door. Sam felt relieved. He'd been worried there wouldn't be enough boxes left; that people like Max, with lots of pocket money, would have bought them all, and that he would miss out.

Steph made a face and a noise as if she was being sick as she passed the Bisky Bricks boxes. She didn't stop but disappeared down an aisle, presumably going to look for containers and notebooks.

'I'll just go and find Uncle Andy,' Sam called after her, carefully sorting through the Bisky Bricks boxes. 'I'll meet you out the front.'

Steph called back 'okay'. Sam looked at the little pictures on the boxes and found three that seemed like they might fit together to form a robot leg. Clutching the boxes, he tore his gaze away from the red swirling robot eyes and walked along the ends of the aisles, looking down each one for Uncle Andy's tall bony figure. He came to the end of the row, skirting a big square basket full of beach balls, and looked down the last aisle. A couple of shoppers with trolleys. A teenager stacking a shelf. But no Uncle Andy.

Sam tried the cool room. The shuddering wintry wind swirled around the rows of MØLK bottles, but the room was empty of people.

Sam edged around a teetering pile of rolls of toilet paper and knocked on the door of Uncle Andy's office. There was no answer, so he opened the door and poked his head in.

'Uncle Andy?' Papers and folders were piled up on the desk; the big whiteboard on the wall was covered with scribbled notes. Bits of gravel lay scattered here and there on the floor, but there was no sign of Uncle Andy.

The lunchroom was also empty.

Out the back, where delivery trucks unloaded,

Sam found piles of boxes and a teenager in a red Magic Mart uniform, but nobody else. No Uncle Andy.

The teenager was unpacking Bisky Bricks boxes from a crate. She turned and stared blankly at Sam.

'Um ... I'm looking for Unc ... for Mr Miller,' Sam said.

The teenage girl looked around the empty loading area as if she expected Uncle Andy to appear suddenly out of thin air. 'Mr Miller,' she said vaguely.

'Yes. Do you know where he is? Have you seen him today?' asked Sam.

'Today?' she said.

'Well, I'll just keep looking,' said Sam, giving up. Uncle Andy always seemed to employ the most hopeless people. 'Maybe he's in the basement ...'

Suddenly the girl said loudly, 'There is nothing in the basement.'

Sam turned back. 'What?'

'There is nothing in the basement,' the girl repeated firmly. She stepped towards him. Her face was still quite blank, and her eyes looked unfocussed and scary. 'There is nothing in the basement,' she said again.

Sam suddenly felt nervous. The back of his

neck prickled. He edged away through the flappy doors into the main part of Magic Mart. 'Err, okay then, thanks,' he said. 'Thanks.'

He walked quickly up the aisle, looking back over his shoulder. She wasn't following him. Sam shuddered, feeling uneasy. There was definitely something weird going on. What was Uncle Andy up to?

The door to the basement was in the far wall at the end of aisle fourteen. It was the aisle for laundry baskets, mops and buckets, sacks of rice and cans of pet food. Sam put his Bisky Bricks boxes down and tried the door handle.

He was surprised that the handle turned. Uncle Andy sometimes used the basement as a storeroom, but usually kept it locked. There was a flight of old concrete stairs with a wooden handrail. The steps went down to a landing, turned, and continued down out of sight. They were dusty and littered with little bits of gravel.

Sam stepped through the door and called, 'Uncle Andy?'

He leaned over the banister and looked down. He could see that there was something there; a faint light was giving off an unusual greenish glow. Sam started down the stairs.

'Uncle Andy?' he called again, a bit louder. 'Are you down there?'

Suddenly, a door slammed below with a metallic clang. Sam jumped.

'Hello?' he said, taking a step back up. 'Uncle Andy?'

The greenish light had disappeared when the door shut, and now the stairs led into darkness. Sam took a few more uncertain steps towards the lighted door at the top. He heard voices below, a key turn in a lock, and then footsteps.

All at once Sam lost his nerve. He scuttled back up the stairs and shot out through the door, back into brightly-lit aisle fourteen. He couldn't have said why, but he had suddenly felt he didn't want to be caught on the stairs. Not even by Uncle Andy. He pushed the door shut, grabbed the three boxes of Bisky Bricks and sprinted down the aisle.

Peering around from behind a stack of brooms, he saw Uncle Andy step out of the door and look around blankly. He didn't see Sam. Then another man appeared. It was the man Sam had seen outside the shop with the dark suit, beard and furry black hat. He said something to Uncle Andy, who looked around again, closed the door very carefully, locked it, and put the keys in his pocket. Then they walked down the aisle away from Sam, towards the front of the store.

Sam felt frozen with surprise. He had never

seen Uncle Andy act in such a suspicious way. What was he doing in the basement? Who was the strange bearded man? What was going on at Magic Mart?

Chapter Seven

Sam collected a plastic shopping basket and took his time choosing the decorations for Molly's outer-space birthday party. With a small part of his mind he was considering what colour balloons and streamers aliens would have at their alien parties. Probably green and silver, he thought, rummaging through a big crate of party supplies. Green was a very alien colour. But most of his thoughts were concentrated on Uncle Andy's strange behaviour. What was he up to? With Uncle Andy, it could be just about anything.

In the cool room there was no normal milk at all. Sam picked up a bottle of MØLK, which seemed the closest thing and, with a basket full of shopping, made his way along to Uncle Andy's office.

'Hey, Uncle Andy,' he said, knocking and poking his head around the open door. 'Hello.'

Uncle Andy looked up. He was sitting behind

his desk, hands resting on the desktop beside an open box of Bisky Bricks. There was no sign of the stranger with the beard. 'Hello,' he said in a flat mechanical voice.

'Umm, Uncle Andy—' Sam took a breath. 'What's happening downstairs? Who's that man with the beard?'

Uncle Andy looked even blanker. His head twitched, his eyes became quite unfocussed and then he said, loudly and firmly, 'There is no man. There is nothing in the basement.'

Sam felt a kind of chill. That was exactly what the girl had said, in exactly the same tone of voice.

'Yes, there is,' Sam insisted. 'I saw him. You were with him. Big black beard like this,' he traced a beard shape with his hands. 'You know. Furry hat. Suit. Who is he?'

'There is no man,' repeated Uncle Andy. He reached over to the box on his desk, took out a Bisky Brick and started to chew it.

'But I saw . . .' said Sam.

'There is no man,' interrupted Uncle Andy in a louder voice, his mouth full.

Sam blinked at him. This was very weird. He felt a sick feeling lodge in the pit of his stomach. He looked into Uncle Andy's blank eyes, trying to understand what he was thinking, but instead he had the horrible sensation that he was looking into the eyes of a stranger. Sam swallowed. *Don't be ridiculous,* he said to himself. *You're imagining things.* Trying to speak normally, trying to shake off the uneasy feeling, he said, 'Well, okay then. Um, Mum says to remind you about Molly's birthday party.'

Uncle Andy twitched his head and his eyes seemed to focus again, but his expression still looked oddly blank. After a pause he said, 'Party.'

'Molly's party,' said Sam. 'You know. On Tuesday.'

'Tuesday,' repeated Uncle Andy. He thought for a second or two, and again said, 'Party.'

Sam was losing patience with this annoying and unsettling conversation. He sucked a breath through his teeth and said, 'Yes. Molly's birthday party. Tuesday. Eleven o'clock. Remember. I'll write it down.'

He leaned over, picked up a pen and wrote: *Molly's party. Tuesday. 11 o'clock. Remember.* on a sticky note on Uncle Andy's desk. He peeled it off, and stuck it in front of him. 'Okay?'

'Okay,' agreed Uncle Andy.

'Good, then,' said Sam. Suddenly he had a brilliant thought. Normally, when Uncle Andy came over he brought something from Magic Mart. Sometimes he brought some weird cheese for Dad, or a packet of chocolate, or biscuits, or something

57

strange, like the time he brought a can of snails, which people apparently eat in France.

'Oh, by the way, Uncle Andy,' he said casually. 'If you were thinking of bringing something along, you know, we're all really loving these Bisky Bricks.' He pointed. 'A great big stack of these would be excellent.'

'Excellent,' said Uncle Andy.

Sam grinned to himself as he went off to find Steph. *Cunning*, he thought.

Paying for his shopping, with Steph hopping from foot to foot impatiently, clutching her new notebooks and sample boxes, Sam looked closely at the teenage boy on the checkout. Was everyone at Magic Mart acting strangely? The boy looked blank and he just said the price and took the money. But that was exactly as usual. How could you tell if someone was behaving in a strange mechanical way when that was how they normally were anyway?

'Bye,' said Sam.

'Bye,' said the teenager in a dull, flat voice.

Back home, Steph returned immediately to digging up the garden and Sam and Moriarty went inside. The house was very quiet. Em had gone to her dancing practice, and Dad was at work. Sam looked around the door of Mum and Dad's bedroom to see Mum and Molly having an afternoon nap. Patrick was curled up on Mum's stomach, like a purring, furry ginger cushion. Sam shut the bedroom door. He tiptoed back into the empty kitchen and put the streamers and balloons in the middle of the table where Mum would find them. He opened the three Bisky Bricks boxes, poured out the Bisky Bricks and quickly found the three new robot parts.

Moriarty started to whine anxiously.

'Shut up,' whispered Sam, chewing on a claggy mouthful and grabbing another handful of Bisky Bricks. 'You'll wake Mum.' He shoved the rest of the Bisky Bricks back into their boxes and tucked them in behind the other boxes on the kitchen counter where Mum maybe wouldn't notice them. 'Come on, dog.'

Sam shut his bedroom door and Moriarty jumped quickly onto the bed. Sam laid the three gleaming, silver robot pieces out on the desk. He took a breath, feeling nervous and slightly sick. He picked up the pieces carefully and turned them over. Just like before, the pieces suddenly moved in his hands. *Click, click, click*, they fitted themselves together. Three wheels surrounded by a caterpillar-track, a streamlined metal strip made of flat, flexible links. Sam gingerly ran his finger along the edge of a wheel. All three wheels spun smoothly and silently, interlocking and frictionless. It was beautiful.

'Wow,' breathed Sam.

Suddenly, without any warning—unless you counted Moriarty's continuous anxious whining—the wheels spun sharply and the leg shot out of Sam's hands, struck the wall behind the desk, ricocheted off at an angle, landed on the floor and sped across the room. It hit the bottom of the bedroom door with a loud, splintering noise and disappeared.

It happened so quickly that, for a second, Sam sat frozen with surprise, gaping at the small jagged hole in the bottom of the bedroom door. Then he sprang up and flung the door open. The passage was empty. There was no sign of the robot leg. A sudden banging noise came from the kitchen. Sam sprinted down the hall. All he could think was that he had to catch the robot leg quickly. Before it destroyed something. Or worse, woke Mum from her afternoon nap.

In the kitchen the robot leg was shooting around the floor, banging off things like an out-of-control pinball. *Thump*, it bashed into the laminex front of a cupboard and shot across the floor in a blur. *Crash*, it dented the front of the fridge and glanced off, speeding under the table with a series of bashing noises as it banged between the legs of the table and chairs. One of the chairs teetered and then toppled over, crashing to the floor.

An angry-sounding voice came from his parents' bedroom.

The robot leg shot out from under the table and Sam dived, full length. His fingers just touched the leg as it sped past, but it was going too fast to catch. Sam crouched, watching the leg zooming and bashing around the kitchen.

He dived again, knocking over another chair, and this time he got his hand on the robot leg. But it shot through his clutching fingers and sped away, bashing hard into the fridge door again, making another dent, then disappeared back under the table. *Bash, bang, thump.*

'Sam? Is that you? What's going on out there?' It was Mum.

'Nothing, nothing,' called Sam.

He got to his feet and tripped over Moriarty, who was pressing up against him anxiously. 'Get out of the way,' said Sam through clenched teeth, trying to keep his eyes on the robot leg.

'Sam, what are you doing?' called Mum. 'I'm coming out.'

'No, no,' yelled Sam, 'Don't worry. I'm just, um, getting a drink—'

He looked around the kitchen. What could

he use? There was a big saucepan sitting on the draining board. Perfect. He dashed across and grabbed it. Just as he turned back, the robot leg thumped into his ankle.

'*Arrrgh!*' he yelled, despite himself, and fell over.

The saucepan rolled away. Moriarty bounded across and started to lick Sam's face. Sam struggled to his feet, pushing Moriarty away, and looked around.

He heard Molly's voice rise in a loud wail. That should slow Mum down for a minute or two. But he had to catch the leg and hide it away. Quickly.

The robot leg was zigzagging in the small space between the fridge and the broom cupboard. *Bang, thump, bang, thump.* Sam limped to the fallen saucepan and picked it up. He measured the distance with his eyes. This time he wasn't going to miss. He stood poised and then, picking the perfect moment, swooped down and plonked the saucepan upside down on top of the robot leg. *Clang, clang, clang,* the robot leg ricocheted around underneath. The saucepan jiggled and jerked. On his hands and knees, Sam grabbed it hard, holding it firmly against the floor, wrapping his arms around it. He put his whole weight on it. He could feel the robot leg bashing from side to side. *Clang, clang, clang.*

Sam looked frantically around the kitchen. What could he do now? His eyes fell on the flat metal oven trays that were stacked in the space between the fridge and the wall. He stretched out an arm but the trays were out of reach. He shoved the saucepan across the floor, keeping as much of his weight on it as he could. He pushed the anxious, whining Moriarty away and pulled out one of the baking trays. The other trays toppled out as well, clattering and banging.

Mum shouted something from the bedroom but Sam was too busy to listen. He lifted one side of the saucepan very slightly off the floor. Not enough to let the leg get out, but enough to poke the edge of the baking tray underneath. Like catching a spider in a jam jar. Then he shoved the whole oven tray under the saucepan.

Holding tightly onto the tray, and feeling like he could do with several extra arms, Sam took a grip on the jerking, clanging saucepan and flipped the whole thing over. There was an extra loud *clang* as the robot leg fell to the bottom.

Sam lifted the tray and peered in. The robot leg was zooming around, banging off the sides, *clang, clang, clang*, but it was trapped. It couldn't get out.

Sam grabbed the saucepan lid from the draining board and slammed it in place, muffling the noise a little. He gave an enormous sigh of relief and sat back, rubbing his bruised ankle.

Molly was still crying. He could hear Mum making shushing noises to her.

'Sam,' she called. 'What are you up to out there? What was all that noise?'

Sam got to his feet and picked up the clanging saucepan. As he carried it to his bedroom he called out, 'Sorry, Mum. Getting a drink. I just knocked over a chair. Sorry. Nothing to worry about.'

Mum muttered suspiciously and Sam heard the bed creak and her determined footsteps on the floor. Sam ducked quickly into his bedroom.

Safely inside, he wrapped the saucepan in his thick winter jacket, which muffled the noise some more, and put it on the floor of his cupboard next to the paint tin. It would be safe there until he got enough parts for a whole robot and was ready to join them all together. He rubbed his hands together happily. He couldn't wait.

Chapter Eight

Sam lay sprawled on his bed, staring blankly up at a patch of light on the ceiling, and chewed a Bisky Brick. He absentmindedly scratched Moriarty's ears, feeling his bruised ankle throbbing. He could still hear the muffled clanging from the bottom of the cupboard where the robot leg was imprisoned in the saucepan, and there was an occasional *snap* from the paint tin. Sam thought about the robot head wrapped in the T-shirt at the back of his sock drawer. He was tempted to get it out, unwrap it, and stare into its eyes again. Could it really hypnotise him? Did it really have some kind of message to deliver? A shiver ran down his back at the thought of those staring red robot eyes. Maybe later.

He tried to work out how many more boxes of Bisky Bricks he would need to complete the robot. One more leg and one more arm, three pieces each, plus however many pieces made up the robot body. Sam glanced across at the picture above his desk. There was no way of telling how many that would be. At least ten more boxes of Bisky Bricks in all, maybe more.

Perhaps Uncle Andy would bring some boxes when he came to Molly's party on Tuesday. Sam hoped very much that he would: he couldn't wait to get more parts. He remembered the enormous pile of Bisky Bricks boxes Max had been buying at Magic Mart. Max had probably nearly finished his model. Maybe Max was playing with a completed robot right now. Sam could just imagine the lovely, shiny silver robot zooming around the floor of Max's bedroom, red eyes flashing and clutching-claw hands snapping.

Sam decided to ring Max and find out how he was going. He tore his gaze away from the ceiling, limped to the kitchen and dialled the number. The phone rang and rang and rang. Sam was just about to give up when it was answered. There was a click and Sam heard someone breathing. After a second or so, he said, 'Err. Hello?'

'Hello,' said a voice.

'Oh, hello,' said Sam. 'Um. Can I talk to Max?'

There was a pause, and then the voice said, 'Max.' The voice was low and expressionless. It didn't sound like Max. Maybe it was a wrong number.

'Oh. I'm sorry. I mean Max from school. This is Sam.'

There was another pause, and the voice said, 'Sam.'

'Is that you, Max? You sound really weird. Are you okay?'

'Okay.'

'Oh, good.' Sam felt a bit uncertain. Maybe Max had a mouth full of Bisky Bricks and that was why he sounded so strange. 'Anyway, I was just wondering how you were getting on with that robot model. I've only got the head and one arm and one leg. How much have you got done? Are you nearly finished?'

'Nearly finished,' said Max.

'Oh really? Your dad hasn't found it, then. What have you got left to collect?'

Max said, 'Nearly finished.'

'Yes,' said Sam. 'What bits do you still need? What parts?'

Max paused as if he was thinking, and then he said, 'One leg. One arm.'

'Wow,' breathed Sam. 'That's excellent. Only one leg and one arm to go? It must be looking good. What are you doing with it?'

After another pause, Max said, 'Follow.'

'What? Where?'

'Follow . . .'

Suddenly there was a struggling noise and a muffled argument. Then a different voice, which Sam recognised straight away as belonging to Max's mum, snapped, 'Who's that?'

'Umm,' he said. 'It's Sam.'

'I'm sorry, Sam,' said Max's mother, sounding more angry than apologetic. 'Max can't talk to you. He's grounded. And he can't use the phone.'

'Can I come around tomorrow?'

'No. Max is grounded for the rest of the holidays.' Max's mum sounded like she wasn't going to say anything else, but then she went on in a rush, 'Maybe forever, in fact. Sam, he smashed up his bedroom furniture, broke the shower screen, and bashed a hole in the wall, for heaven's sake. I don't know what his father will say.' She sounded as if she thought Sam was also to blame. Then she gave a despairing groan, sniffed furiously and hung up the phone.

Sam was left listening to the dial tone. He put down the receiver.

What was Max playing at? He'd collected almost all the parts he needed for the robot. If Sam were in Max's place, he wouldn't be wasting such an amazing model by just following it around like an idiot. That was for sure.

Max's mother hadn't mentioned the robot, but if it was destroying Max's house, then his parents would surely find it soon and take it away from him. And Sam knew people's parents talked to each other. All the time. Max's mum would talk to Sam's mum about the robot, and then Sam wouldn't be allowed to keep his either.

Sam rubbed his ankle and thought about the unfairness in the world. He'd like to have seen Max's nearly finished robot, and he wondered if Max would manage to sneak out and get enough Bisky Bricks to finish the model. Maybe not.

Sam felt a bit sorry for Max; he only needed a few more parts, and now it looked like Sam would finish his robot first, after all.

He cheerfully munched up another Bisky Brick.

Em returned home angry from dancing class. She stamped into the kitchen and emptied a shopping bag onto the table. A sparkling rainbow cascaded out, made up of glittering beads, tiny mirrors and packets of sequins. Some of the beads rolled right across the table and scattered onto the floor.

'What's going on?' asked Sam, dazzled by the pile of tiny sparkling things and using his arms to stop the rest of the beads from trickling off the edge of the table. 'Stop that, Moriarty. They're not for eating.' Moriarty looked up guiltily.

'Stupid old dog,' said Sam, picking the sequins out of the hair around Moriarty's mouth and giving him a pat on the head. Moriarty sneezed, and some tiny beads shot out of his nose. Sam laughed.

'That Ms Prance,' snapped Em, pulling her pink costume out of her bag. 'She's made me a soloist, but she's made that Bethany a soloist too. Now we're going to have to dance together. *Euugh.* I'm going to have to dance a duet with Be-tha-ny.' Em did her imitation of Bethany: a stupid smile and a posturing, bottom-poking-out pose. 'But,' she went on firmly, 'no way is darling Bethany going to have all the attention. Her costume is sparkly. But mine is going to be sparklier. Much, much sparklier. Next to me, people won't even notice she's on the stage.'

Em sat down at the table and pulled out a reel of cotton and a packet of needles. She bit off a length of thread, licked the end and threaded a needle. She picked up a packet of tiny mirrors. They caught the light, glinting and flashing. Sam stared at them, dazzled.

Em started to sew the little mirrors around the neckline of her costume. She sewed quickly, stabbing the needle into the sparkly pink fabric and singing angrily under her breath through clenched teeth.

'*Sparkle, sparkle, night and day,*
Perfect as a perfect rose,
Sparkle each and every way,
Sparkling feet and twinkling toes.'

Moriarty started to howl enthusiastically. Em glared and said, 'Don't just sit there, Sam. Make that stupid dog shut up, and give me a hand.' She pushed a packet of silver sequins and the needles and thread across to him. 'Come on.'

Luckily for Sam, who didn't like sewing at all, and who was feeling sick from hearing the horrible song, at that moment Mum came in carrying Molly. Molly was enchanted by all the sparkly things, and under cover of the chaos of Em shouting, trying to stop the beads trickling onto the floor and trying to keep Molly away, and Molly yelling and grabbing, and Mum trying to calm both of them down, Sam and Moriarty slunk away. Sam had been going to tell Mum about Uncle Andy's strange behaviour at Magic Mart, but that could wait.

Sunday dinner was Sam's favourite meal of the week because it was always fish and chips.

As he walked along the street to collect the hot, heavy, delicious parcel, Sam was annoyed to find he was humming the tune of Em's 'Sparkle,

sparkle' song. He'd heard it once too often and now it was stuck in his head. He looked around. There were a few people in the street but no one was close enough to overhear, which was a relief. Then he looked down at Moriarty and saw something glinting on the top of his head. Sam stopped and looked more closely. It was a tiny silver sequin, sparkling in the sunshine. Horrified, he picked it off and flicked it away. What if he'd turned up at the fish and chip shop with a dog covered in sequins and started singing 'Sparkle, sparkle'? He went red just thinking about it.

While he was waiting for the fish and chips, being very careful not to hum anything, half listening to the chatter of the other waiting people, Sam suddenly heard part of a conversation. Two ladies near the drinks fridge were talking about the mysterious lights in the sky, and one of them said, '. . . this afternoon. I saw it shoot right out of that weird old supermarket on the cliff. You know. Just like that—' she zoomed her hand through the air and made a *whoosh* noise.

Right out of Magic Mart, thought Sam. Things were getting stranger and stranger. What was Uncle Andy up to?

Chapter Nine

In between mouthfuls of chips and Bisky Bricks, Sam told Mum and Dad about Uncle Andy's odd behaviour, his strange new voice, and his mysterious activities in the basement at Magic Mart. 'I think something really weird's going on,' said Sam. 'And in the fish and chip shop—'

Dad was rolling his eyes and looking annoyed. Suddenly he exclaimed, 'What's he up to now? Something foolish, I suppose. Did I tell you kids about the time he wanted to make a swimming pool in our bedroom?'

'Yes,' said Sam, Em and Steph all together.

Dad carried on regardless. 'Do you know what he did? He shut the door of the bedroom and put the hose in through the window and turned the tap on. He thought we'd have a pool in there. He thought we'd just swim around the bedroom. The whole house was flooded. Your nan was absolutely livid. I'd never seen her so angry, ha ha ha.'

'Did you remind him about Molly's birthday, Sam?' asked Mum.

'Yes, and I wrote it down,' said Sam, feeding a chip into Moriarty's waiting mouth. 'Anyway I want to tell you . . .'

'Don't feed that dog at the table,' said Dad.

'So, two days to go,' said Mum, looking at the birthday party list and forking up a chip. Mum was the only person Sam knew who ate fish and chips with a knife and fork. It was one of her things. 'Tomorrow I'll make the cake. Will you decorate it, Em? I thought we'd do it in the shape of a UFO. What do you think?'

Em said, 'Sure. Okay.'

'You know,' said Sam, forgetting the mysterious lights for a moment. 'A UFO is an Unidentified Flying Object. It could be anything, a comet or a bird, even.'

'Or a firefly. Or a wasp,' said Steph.

'Okay,' agreed Mum. 'An alien spaceship cake, then.'

'Did you know,' said Steph suddenly, 'there's a kind of wasp that when it lays its eggs, it gets a caterpillar and paralyses it and leaves it right there, so that when the eggs hatch, the baby wasps can eat up the fresh caterpillar straight away, while it's still alive? Imagine if we lived like that? Imagine that.'

Everyone stopped eating. Even Molly stopped pulling chips to bits for a second. Sam imagined the caterpillar, alive and paralysed, being eaten up by the baby wasps. He lowered the chip he had been about to stuff into his mouth.

'And do you know how flies eat?' Steph went on. 'They can't even chew. They haven't got teeth, they've just got this straw to suck things up through. So they vomit on the food, and the vomit dissolves the food, and then they just suck it up.' Steph made a sucking noise to illustrate the fly's table manners. 'Isn't that interesting?'

Mum swallowed, frowned and said, 'Steph, what did we agree about mealtime conversation?'

'What?' protested Steph. 'What? You said nothing disgusting. That's not disgusting. That's interesting.'

'It's definitely disgusting,' said Em, looking pale.

'It's not disgusting,' said Steph indignantly. 'I'll tell you something disgusting. Did you know, when the praying mantis—'

'No!' said Dad, pointing a finger.

'Enough, Steph,' said Mum. 'Not while we're eating.'

Steph subsided into a sulky silence. Sam was relieved. Steph had told him about the praying mantis before, and he didn't want to hear any more stomach-churning insect facts. He fed his last few chips to Moriarty and watched Dad get up, put the kettle on and walk over to open the fridge.

Before dinner Sam had fixed the hole in his bedroom door by carefully gluing a piece of cardboard over it. He'd coloured the cardboard brown to match the door. You could see where it was, but only if you looked very closely. There wasn't much he could do about the dents that the robot leg had made in the fridge, though. The best thing he could think of was to move some of Molly's artwork down to cover them and hope that Dad wouldn't notice. The fridge was Dad's pride and joy. It was new, a Chilltastic RV, very white and shiny and efficient.

Fortunately, Dad didn't look too closely at the fridge door. He patted Patrick, who was eating his piece of fish safely up on top of the fridge. He grabbed a packet of chocolate sultanas, which he handed to Mum. He picked up the purple bottle of MØLK, opened it and sniffed it. '*Eugh.* What is this?' He read the label, put the bottle back, closed the fridge, and said, 'Black coffee, I think,' and went over to the coffee pot.

Sam silently let out the breath he had been holding.

'Lovely,' said Mum, opening up the sultanas. 'Now. Tomorrow. There's lots to do. We have to tidy up the house so it'll be ready for the party.

We've got to plan the games. And you've all got your costumes to sort out.'

Em held out her hand for sultanas. 'I'm going to wear my dancing costume,' she announced. 'It's going to look amazing. It's going to be covered with sequins and mirrors and I'm going to sew on those flashing Christmas lights. It'll look really, really sparkly. I'm going to come as a star. I'm going to have the sparkliest costume, I bet.'

'No doubt about that,' said Mum, with half a smile. 'That's good, then. What about you, Steph?'

Steph was lining her chocolate sultanas up in a row and then eating them one by one. She shrugged.

'Come on, darling,' said Mum. 'You could dress up as an alien, or as an astronaut. Or maybe an insect or something?'

Steph shrugged again, catching her sultanas as they rolled away and bringing them back into line.

Dad said, 'Look at that. Looks like the table's crooked.'

They all watched Steph's chocolate sultanas rolling gently across the table. Sam noticed some of his were doing the same. Dad reached out and grabbed both sides of the table top to see if the legs were firm on the floor. 'That's odd,' he said. 'It feels solid enough.' He squinted, turning his head to the side.

Sam said, 'Em, your beads kept trickling off the table this afternoon, didn't they?'

'Yes, that's right. And then your stupid dog ate them up,' said Em, glaring at Moriarty.

'He's not stupid,' said Sam, patting Moriarty comfortingly on the head. 'He's very clever.'

Em laughed rudely. 'Clever!' she said. 'He's the stupidest dog—'

Mum interrupted, 'Quiet, Em. Now, Sam. What about your costume?'

Sam made a face at Em and explained to Mum about the bike helmet and the silver foil and the ping-pong balls. Em snorted scornfully.

'That sounds great,' said Mum. 'Could you help Steph make something like that, too, Sam? How would that be, Steph?'

'Sure,' said Sam.

'Okay,' said Steph reluctantly.

'Good,' said Mum, crossing *costumes* off her party list with a flourish. 'That's sorted, then.'

Dad was glaring at the table, turning his head from side to side. Sam couldn't help wondering if the robot leg bashing into the table had somehow made it crooked. He couldn't see how, though. He tried to look unconcerned.

Dad said, 'I'll just go and get the spirit level, I think.'

Sam suddenly remembered the lights in the

sky. 'Oh, Dad. I forgot. These ladies in the fish and chip shop said they saw one of those mysterious lights shoot right out of Magic Mart.'

Dad looked at him with a frown. 'That little brother of mine. What's he up to now? What's he doing?' He glared. 'Something stupid, no doubt. You know, he's probably making fireworks in that basement. And shooting them off into the sky. And now everyone's talking about aliens.' He made an aggravated, growling noise in his throat.

'He's been really weird for ages,' said Em.

Dad gave an enormous, exasperated sigh. He suddenly slapped the table, making them all jump. 'That's it,' he said. 'This has gone far enough. I'm going to get to the bottom of it. Whatever mad thing he's up to, I'll find out. He's probably doing something really stupid and dangerous. I'll go and have a word with him. Right now.'

Sam followed him into the hallway. 'Can I come?'

'No, Sam. Not this time.' Dad waved him back and left the house, slamming the front door.

Dad didn't often slam doors. Sam turned back, disappointed. He would have liked to go with Dad and find out what Uncle Andy was up to. Maybe find out what was in the basement at Magic Mart. As Dad said, Uncle Andy was prob- ably shooting fireworks into the sky for some reason. He'd like to have seen the fireworks. They must be amazing.

The next morning Sam was lying half-awake, squashed against the wall because Moriarty liked to sleep stretched out across the bed. He listened to the muffled clanging noise from the saucepan in the cupboard, and Moriarty's answering, sleepy growls. He was thinking, vaguely, about the lights in the sky and he suddenly realised that the light he had seen two days before, when he had been standing in the back garden, must have been flying *towards* Magic Mart, not away from it. With his eyes shut, he tried to remember exactly. He and Steph had been walking back towards the house. He'd looked up, and the light had shot across the sky—from behind the house, over the back fence, down towards the sea. Towards Magic Mart. He was sure of it.

He sat up with a jerk. Whatever the lights were, they couldn't be fireworks coming from Magic Mart. He needed to tell Dad straight away. He crawled across Moriarty and scrambled out of bed.

In the kitchen, Mum was on her hands and knees rummaging at the back of a cupboard and Molly was in her high chair, slopping a spoon in a bowl of mushy cereal.

'Where's Dad?' asked Sam.

'You're up early,' said Mum. 'He's gone to see Uncle Andy before work. He couldn't find him last night, so he's going to catch him at Magic Mart this morning. You haven't seen that big saucepan, have you?'

'I've got to tell him something,' said Sam. 'Those lights, they can't be fireworks.' He explained about the light he'd seen in the back garden. 'I've got to tell Dad,' he repeated.

'You can tell him tonight,' said Mum. She picked up a list from the table and looked at it, pen hovering. 'Now you're up, Sam, you can choose: hang up the washing or clean the windows?'

Sam wished he had stayed in bed. He sighed. 'Can I at least eat breakfast first?'

'If you're quick,' said Mum briskly.

It was going to be one of those days, Sam could tell.

Chapter Ten

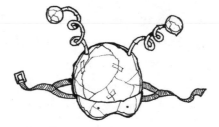

That morning Sam found himself hanging up washing and then cleaning windows. Followed by scrubbing the bathroom floor, eating a very fast lunch and tidying the laundry. Then listening to Mum arguing with Em, saying Em should stop sewing sequins and flashing lights onto her costume, that it was sparkly enough and that she should give a hand with the housework.

So then Sam helped a sulky Em move the furniture around in the lounge room so she could vacuum, and then moved it all back again. After that, exhausted from housework, he escaped from Mum's list and slunk away to his bedroom with the bike helmet, silver foil, wire, scissors, ping-pong balls and a big roll of packing tape. Moriarty, who hated cleaning and furniture moving, and who had been snapped at by Mum for getting under her feet, was curled up on Sam's bed, head turned to the wall. Sam gave him a comforting pat, cleared a space on the floor, and sat down to construct his costume for the party.

It took a while, and when he was finished the bedroom was covered with little bits of silver foil and sticky tape, but the alien helmet looked excellent. Sam had added a silver-foil visor, which came down over his eyes and the top part of his face. He was pretty certain that this looked amazing and alien-like, but he couldn't tell for sure, because when he was wearing it, he couldn't see his reflection in the bathroom mirror. He could only see part of the sparkling-clean, well-scrubbed tile floor and part of the wall. If he tilted his head right back, he could see a silver gleam in the mirror, but that was all.

He made two tiny holes in the visor with the point of the scissors. Now he could sort of see. Especially when he moved his head from side to side. Then he could see almost everything, a bit at a time. He wagged his head, admiring the way the two antennae—made from the ping-pong balls attached to the ends of long pieces of curling wire and covered with silver foil—waved in a convincing, alien manner.

Sam gave his reflection a weird, alien smile, showing his teeth, and then went to look for Steph.

She had dug up a lot of the back garden. One

trench burrowed right under the house. Another one, crossing the first, stretched almost from one side of the garden to the other. There were smaller holes and piles of dirt and rocks everywhere. With his visor on, Sam had to watch carefully where he walked so he didn't fall into anything. He looked into all the holes and behind the larger piles of dirt, but Steph was nowhere to be seen. Sam went back inside.

Mum was taking a cake out of the oven. It smelled delicious. Sam's mouth watered.

'Look at that,' she said, holding out the hot cake tin. Sam squinted through the visor, turning his head from side to side until the cake came into view. The cake was sloping as if it had been cooked on an angle. 'I've never had a cake come out like that before,' said Mum, sounding annoyed. 'I'll have to cut the top off flat to level it out.' She looked up at Sam and his alien helmet. 'Oh, that looks really good, Sam. Well done you. Can you see at all?'

'I can see everything,' said Sam. 'Just not all at once. Where's Steph?'

'Getting the washing in.' Mum smiled at him, and then went back to frowning at her cake.

Steph wasn't actually getting the washing in. Sam went down the side of the house to the washing line and, after peering around for a while, found her standing quite still, staring intently at a hanging towel.

She turned around, saw his helmet, and grinned. 'That looks really cool, Sam. Can you see? Are you going to make me one like that?'

'If you like,' he said. 'What are you doing?'

'Just watching this.' She pointed.

Sam peered through the visor. There was a tiny green caterpillar making its way up the towel. Steph scrutinised it for a few more seconds, then gently collected it onto a finger and carried it across to a geranium plant next to the house.

'Steph,' said Sam, watching her encourage the caterpillar onto a leaf. 'You know that light we saw in the back garden?' Steph nodded. 'Do you remember which way it went?'

Steph thought for a second and shrugged. 'No, I didn't really see it at all. Not properly.'

'It was going that way,' said Sam, turning around to get his bearings and pointing. 'Towards Magic Mart. So it can't be fireworks set off by Uncle Andy. It was going the wrong way.'

Steph frowned. 'Well, you saw another one, didn't you? On the foreshore? Which way was that one going?'

Sam tried to remember. He'd been spinning around at the time, so it was hard to say for sure.

'I think . . .' he stopped. 'I think it was going away from Magic Mart,' he said finally.

'So, someone saw something shooting out of Magic Mart,' Steph said, 'and you saw something shooting towards it and away from it. So maybe there's something flying around, all over the place, or maybe something's coming and going from Magic Mart.'

Sam looked into what he could see of Steph's puzzled face. What kind of thing could be coming and going from Magic Mart like that?

Steph liked her silver alien helmet so much she wore it at dinnertime. It was funny to watch her trying to eat soup without really being able to see it, with the two silver antennae waving every time she moved her head. Sam offered to make one for Molly as well, but Mum said better not.

'It's her very first birthday party,' she said, smiling at Molly. 'It'd be nice if she could see it happen.'

Sam and Steph both giggled.

'I could make something for Moriarty, then,' said Sam, patting him on the head. 'You can be an alien dog. I bet aliens have weird dogs.'

'Not as weird as him, though, I bet,' said Em rudely.

Sam made a face at her.

'Em, stop sewing now. It's dinnertime,' said Mum.

Em pushed her costume aside. Sam found he was staring at it. He couldn't take his eyes off it: it was dazzling. As far as Sam could tell, there wasn't an un-sparkly space left, and now there was a string of twinkling Christmas lights as well. Em had attached the battery pack to the back. When she switched the lights on, the costume was so glittery it was painful to look at without squinting.

Em was singing the horrible 'Sparkle, sparkle' song.

'*Sparkle, sparkle, glint and shine,*
Sparkle sparkle, through and through,
Twinkle like a diamond mine,
Glitter like a drop of dew.'

'Not with your mouth full, Em,' said Mum. 'Sam, eat up, don't just stare into space.'

Sam jumped and blinked. He felt dazed. He reached out and sprinkled bits of Bisky Brick into his soup.

'Oh, Sam,' said Mum. 'Mrs Colefax, next door, was telling me about some kind of dangerous toy her nephew, Pete, was building. It attacked him, she said. He had to have stitches, apparently. That wouldn't be the same thing you're making, would it?'

Sam gulped. 'Um, no. No,' he said. 'No, of course not. No. Mine's just a little model.' *Stitches*, he thought to himself. He'd have to be careful.

'I'll get your dad to have a look at it, I think,' said Mum. 'Just to be on the safe side.'

Sam swallowed. 'Where *is* Dad?'

'He rang up to say he's working late,' said Mum, still looking at him as if she thought he was up to something. 'I don't know when he'll be home.'

'Oh.' Sam was disappointed.

Mum saw his expression. 'Don't worry,' she said. 'He's promised to take tomorrow off for the party. We'll have him here at home all day.'

When Sam got up the next morning, the house looked strange and unfamiliar because of all the housework. Em was decorating Molly's birthday cake and Dad was standing, drinking coffee, chewing something, and staring blankly at the wall. Moriarty bounded across to him and looked up hopefully but Dad ignored him.

'Hey, Sam,' said Em. 'Look at this.'

Sam looked. The cake was very impressive. It was the shape of a flying saucer, and Em had decorated it with green swirly icing. Now she was adding a row of chocolate buttons along the side.

'That looks amazing,' said Sam. He sneaked a chocolate button from where it had rolled to the edge of the table and secretly ate it. 'Dad, did you see Uncle Andy yesterday? Did you find out what he's up to?'

'What he's up to,' repeated Dad, doing a really good Uncle Andy imitation, blank expression and all.

Sam laughed, looking for orange juice in the fridge. 'That's exactly what he sounds like. And did you talk to him? Did you find out what's going on?'

'What's going on,' repeated Dad in the same voice.

Em rolled her eyes. 'He's been like this all morning,' she said. 'It stops being funny after a while.'

'But Dad,' said Sam, 'did you go down into the basement? And did you see that man, the strange man with the suit and the beard?'

'There is nothing in the basement,' said Dad firmly.

Suddenly Sam felt sick. Not Dad as well. Surely he must be joking. Sam swallowed. 'Oh, but seriously, Dad, I need to tell you something. You know those lights?'

'There are no lights in the sky,' interrupted Dad.

'What? Of course there are,' said Sam. 'But, Dad . . .'

'There you are, Sam.' Mum rushed in from outside with Molly on her hip. She grabbed the coffee pot. 'Molly's birthday!' she announced, jiggling Molly and pouring coffee.

'Oh, yeah, of course,' said Sam. 'Happy Birthday, Molly.' He pulled a bug-eyed face at Molly to make her laugh and then gave her a quick peck on the cheek. 'Happy Birthday.'

'Em, that's looking lovely,' said Mum, admiring the birthday cake and holding firmly onto Molly who was squealing like a fire engine and looked like she wanted to dive right into it. Em gave her a chocolate button.

'I didn't hear you come in last night,' said Mum to Dad, adding MØLK to her coffee. 'You must've been very late.'

'Very late,' agreed Dad.

'Did you talk to Andy? Is he all right?'

'All right,' said Dad.

'Oh, that's good. Now, can you carry these chairs out to the front garden? And set up the trestle-table?'

Dad put down his coffee cup, picked up a chair and wandered out with it.

'And Sam,' Mum went on. 'Balloons, yes? And streamers?' She pointed at the pile of decorations on the counter. 'Where's Steph? She might give you a hand.'

Sam nodded. 'Mum, Dad's acting really weird. Is he okay, do you think?'

'Okay?' Mum slurped her coffee and pulled a face. '*Eugh!* What is this?' She plonked the cup into the sink and zoomed out of the kitchen with Molly, who now had smears of chocolate all over her hands and face. 'As far as I know,' she said over her shoulder.

Sam sat down at the table. His legs were feeling shaky and weak. What was going on? Dad had gone to see what Uncle Andy was up to, and now he'd come back talking in this frightening way. What was happening in the basement at Magic Mart? He'd have to go himself, he thought, and find out. He looked across at Dad's breakfast plate and he felt a cold feeling suddenly lodge deep in his stomach.

Normally, Dad ate toast for breakfast. He always ate toast. But the crumbs on Dad's plate weren't toast crumbs.

They were Bisky Brick crumbs.

Chapter Eleven

After breakfast, Sam tried to catch Mum's attention as she charged around with a list, ticking things off. 'Mum, Dad's acting really strangely,' he said. 'He was eating Bisky Bricks this morning, and he said he hated them. And Uncle Andy's getting weirder, too. There's something going on at Magic Mart. In the basement. Something creepy.'

Mum paused as she raced past. 'What? Have you made a start with those balloons yet, Sam?'

'Listen, Mum,' said Sam. 'Uncle Andy said, "There's nothing in the basement" in this really weird voice. Like that. And then, today, Dad said it. "There's nothing in the basement".'

Mum frowned. 'Well, that's good, isn't it?' she said, looking at her list. 'Sausage rolls, party pies,' she muttered to herself. 'Chips. Fruit. Drinks. Sam, please move this foolish dog, I keep tripping over him.'

'It's important, Mum,' said Sam, pulling

Moriarty out of Mum's way. 'Something's happened to Dad. And Uncle Andy. Really.'

Mum glanced at him.

'Really,' said Sam.

Mum looked at her watch and sighed. 'That Uncle Andy. What's he up to now? I don't want him dragging your dad into any of his mad schemes. Look, Sam, there's no time now, but after the party, I'll go down to Magic Mart with you. We'll find out what's going on. Don't worry. It'll probably turn out to be just some foolish thing of Uncle Andy's. Okay?'

'Okay,' agreed Sam. He felt relieved. Mum was good at getting to the bottom of things. She'd work out what was going on. After the party, they'd find out what was happening in the basement at Magic Mart.

'Good,' he said to himself. He reached out for a Bisky Brick, but then something made him stop. He thought of Dad and Uncle Andy both eating Bisky Bricks. He drew his hand back. *No*, he thought. *No more for the moment. Not until we know.*

Sam blew up green balloons until he felt dizzy, tied them in bunches with string, and stuck them up around the house and the front garden. Steph unrolled the streamers, twisted the silver and green together, then looped them back and forth around the lounge room, around the kitchen and in and out of the trees outside.

Em put the final touches to the birthday cake. There was one big candle in the middle—because Molly was turning one—and Em had added extra little candles around the edges.

Dad carried chairs outside, set up the trestle-table in the front garden under the apple tree, and laid out the tablecloth. He didn't say much at all, as if his attention was somewhere else.

'Nearly eleven,' said Mum, ticking the last thing off her list. 'People will be arriving any minute.'

By a quarter past, there were crowds of people milling about the front garden. Little kids like Molly were being carried around, screaming and wailing. Older kids were running around and yelling, dressed up like aliens and astronauts. Adults stood in bunches, talking.

Sam had put on his alien helmet, so he could only see small parts of things. A four-year-old running past, laughing, her face painted green to look like a Martian. A balloon flying away. A small boy with a silver-painted ice-cream container on his head, looking bewildered. A blinding flash from Em's dancing costume, which was even sparklier out in the sunshine. Grass. Sky. Moriarty's sparkling silver-foil alien collar and waving tail.

Seeing the party in bits like this made Sam feel strange and separate.

Mum helped Molly unwrap her presents. Molly enjoyed the coloured wrapping paper and the ribbons as much as the presents themselves. She sat on the grass surrounded by torn paper and plastic toys, yelling happily and waving her hands about.

Steph wasn't being any help because, like Sam, she was wearing her alien helmet and so she couldn't see much. Sam had a glimpse of her tripping over a toddler and sprawling full-length on the grass. Sam snorted, and just then, as he moved his head from side to side, he caught sight of Uncle Andy at the front gate.

'Uncle Andy,' he called. He went to meet him, trying not to fall over anyone. Uncle Andy turned. His arms were full of boxes. He looked blank. He didn't seem to recognise Sam.

'It's me. Sam,' said Sam. He tilted his head back to get a better look at Uncle Andy's face, and got a glimpse of the boxes he was carrying. He gasped. He could hardly believe his eyes. Uncle Andy had a huge pile, maybe twenty boxes, of Bisky Bricks.

'Sam?' said Uncle Andy.

'Yes, it's me,' said Sam. 'Wow. Bisky Bricks. Amazing. Are they for me? Can I have them?'

'Have them,' said Uncle Andy.

'Really? Wow!' said Sam again, clutching the teetering stack of boxes. 'Thanks, Uncle Andy. This is amazing.'

'Amazing,' agreed Uncle Andy.

All thoughts about Molly's birthday party, Dad's strange behaviour, the mysterious lights and Uncle Andy's secret at Magic Mart went out of Sam's head. All he could think about was the beautiful silver robot. Maybe there'd be enough pieces in these boxes to finish the model. Then he'd have an actual killer robot of his own, zooming around the house, snapping its clutching-claw hands and flashing its glowing red eyes. He couldn't wait. Awkwardly clasping the pile of boxes, he rushed inside to his bedroom and shut the door.

He'd got quite used to the alien helmet, and he liked the way the world appeared a little bit at a time. Everything looked different. In the kitchen, for example, the floor looked like it was sloping downhill.

But maybe it might be better if he could see what he was doing while he was building the robot, so he took the helmet off and perched it on the end of the bed. He emptied the Bisky Brick boxes onto the bedspread and scrabbled through the seaweedy pile, picking out the robot parts. A clutching-claw robot hand nipped at his finger.

He grabbed it. There were new smooth, shiny, squarish pieces and a couple of leg parts. He carried them to his desk and laid them all out in a long row.

Outside the party was still going. Little kids yelling. Moriarty barking. Sam thought he could hear Em singing the 'Sparkle, sparkle' song. From the cupboard there came a muffled *clang, clang, clang.* And from somewhere in the house there was a creaking noise.

Sam swallowed. There was a nervous feeling in his stomach and an odd ringing in his ears.

Sam didn't try to join the robot pieces together straight away. This time, he had a plan. He collected the saucepan and the paint can from the floor of the cupboard. He took the lid off the saucepan and watched the robot leg zooming back and forth, banging off the sides. It didn't seem to have slowed down at all during its two days in the cupboard. He prised the lid off the paint can with a pen. *Snap. Snap.* The robot arm was writhing angrily inside, surrounded by little torn bits of gardening glove. Sam cautiously tilted the can, keeping his fingers well away from the edge, to tip the robot arm and the glove confetti in with the robot leg. The snapping claw grabbed at the rim of the can, but missed. It fell into the saucepan with a *clunk.*

The robot leg paused for a tiny second, and then carried on zigzagging. The robot arm snapped at the leg as it shot past. Sam put the lid carefully on the clanging saucepan. Now he had an empty paint can, which would be just the thing to build the new robot parts in. If he made them inside the can, then they wouldn't be able to escape.

It worked really well. First he picked out three pieces to make another arm. Holding them inside the paint can, he turned them around until he felt the familiar, *click, click* as the pieces fitted themselves together. The finished arm writhed in his fingers, snapping its clutching claw, and Sam dropped it neatly and safely into the bottom of the paint tin. Then he picked up the tin and tipped the twisting, snapping arm into the saucepan to join the other pieces. The two arms squabbled briefly, snapping at each other. The robot leg kept zooming back and forth. Sam put the lid back on.

He examined the pieces on the desk, careful to keep them separate. He didn't want anything to happen before he was ready. He picked out three pieces that would make another robot leg and just like before—*click, click, click*—they joined themselves together. Before the completed leg could shoot out of his hands, he dropped it safely into the paint tin. It started zooming around straight away. Sam tilted the tin to empty the leg into the saucepan. But with a sudden burst of speed the leg shot out of the tin, skipped along the rim of the saucepan, and zoomed across the floor. *Bang*, it hit the metal leg of the bed and shot back towards where Sam was sitting at the desk.

Sam flung himself off the chair and slammed the paint tin upside down on top of the speeding robot leg. *Clang, clang, clang.* He'd caught it. He gasped for breath. He could feel his heart thumping. After a moment he reached out and grabbed a school folder from beneath the bed. He shoved the folder under the paint tin, flipped the tin back over, and carefully, very carefully, emptied the robot leg into the saucepan with the other finished robot limbs.

There were about fourteen parts left on the desk. Sam examined them cautiously. He recognised a number of them as bits of arms or legs or head. There were four pieces he hadn't seen before. He'd already made two arms and two legs and the head. So these four parts must be the robot body. He looked at the picture above the desk. The robot's body was solid-looking and rectangular. The four pieces on the desk were also rectangular. Sam picked them up and, holding them over the paint tin, tried to fit them together.

He turned them this way and that way. He turned them around. He flipped them over. Suddenly they moved in his hands, and with the familiar *click, click, click* they fitted themselves together to form a silver robot body.

Sam dropped it into the paint tin and waited to see what it would do. But it just lay there, gleaming. Sam fished it out again and examined it. It was so smooth he couldn't see where the four pieces had joined. There were sockets where the head and the arms and legs would connect. He could feel a faint buzzing through his fingertips. He held it up to his ear. A slight hum.

He reached down and took the lid off the saucepan. The two arms were snapping at each other and the two legs were clanging from side to side.

Sam lowered the robot body into the saucepan. He kept hold of it and poked it towards one of the speeding legs. *Click.* The leg connected itself into a socket. The robot body shot out of his hand and went clanging wildly and lopsidedly around the saucepan. Sam gasped. *Click.* The other leg connected itself in place. The robot spun like a top, and then started zooming around in a small circle. The two arms snapped at it like angry snakes, twisting and jumping.

Two more clicks, and suddenly the arms

were attached to the shoulder sockets. *Snap, snap, snap!* The robot body flexed its new arms, twirled them around. It snapped its clutching-claw hands. It banged around the saucepan, crashing and snapping. It reached up an arm, trying to grab the rim of the saucepan. Sam slammed the lid down.

'Wow,' he breathed.

The robot was beautiful. So shiny and silver. So fast. So snappy. All it needed was the head.

It felt like an important moment. The head was still wrapped up at the back of his sock drawer. Sam remembered the hypnotising effect of its eyes. He picked up the alien helmet from the bed. He hoped he would be safer with the helmet on because it made it impossible for him to look at anything directly. The robot wouldn't be able to stare into his eyes and wouldn't be able to hypnotise him.

He pulled out the robot head from the sock drawer and unwrapped it. The red eyes were still glowing but, with the helmet on, Sam was only getting little glances from them, not a steady stare. His head felt dizzy and strange, but it wasn't like before. The red eyes didn't try to invade his brain.

Carefully, he lifted the lid off the saucepan and lowered the head onto the clanging, snapping body. *Click.* It was in place. The robot stopped. It went quiet.

At last it was complete.

Then it turned its head and looked up at him.

Chapter Twelve

Sam gazed down at the robot through the visor of his alien helmet. All at once, the party noises outside seemed very distant. The robot stood motionless in the saucepan. It was humming. Its red eyes were glowing. It stared up at Sam. Sam could tell it was trying to hypnotise him again. His head started to swim. But looking at it through the holes in the visor was definitely protecting him. Instead of seeming to get bigger and bigger and surrounding him, the robot's eyes stayed small.

But they glowed more brightly, as if it was frustrated. The robot's humming began to sound shrill and annoyed. Sam felt very dizzy and light-headed, but he wasn't losing himself this time. The robot couldn't get right inside his head. With an effort, he dragged his gaze away from the robot's glowing eyes and took a gasping breath.

Now he could hear the party again. People had

started to sing 'Happy birthday'. They must be cutting the cake.

'Wow.' He leaned back.

The robot's head swivelled, its gaze following him. It really was beautiful. Shiny and silver and sleek.

Sam picked up a plastic ruler from the desk and cautiously reached it towards the robot, trying not to look it in the eyes. He gently tapped one of the clutching-claw hands. The robot's head turned to watch the ruler. The red eyes glowed. Sam tapped it again.

With a speed that made him jump, the robot suddenly snatched the ruler. Sam gasped and jerked back. The robot grabbed the ruler in its other claw, bent it like a banana, let it spring back, then spun it around, fast enough to make a blur. It balanced the ruler upright on one hand, then flipped it end over end and caught it on the other hand. For a second, Sam felt like applauding.

But then the robot backed up, holding one end of the ruler in both hands, and stuck the other end against the bottom of the saucepan. It flexed the ruler again and bent it into a tight curve. Then *sproing*, like a pole vaulter, the robot flipped itself into the air. It somersaulted out of the saucepan, right over Sam's head.

Sam gasped, ducked, twisted around and lost his balance. The chair tipped over and he fell onto the floor. The alien helmet came off his head and rolled under the bed.

Sam scrambled to his hands and knees, untangling himself from the chair, and tried to see where the robot had landed. He peered all around the floor, under the desk, under the bed. Nothing.

He listened. They'd stopped singing outside. The party must be nearly over. He thought he could hear the robot humming but he couldn't tell where the noise was coming from. Where could it have landed? He looked more carefully. Under a biggish pile of clothes. In the corner beside the cupboard. Behind the empty saucepan.

Still looking around, he got to his knees. Suddenly he was face to face with it, only centimetres away. The robot had catapulted from the saucepan onto the top of the desk. And it was waiting for him, humming, on the edge of the desktop, red eyes glowing brightly.

Sam shrank back but it was already too late. He tried to drag his gaze away. He tried to bring up a hand to cover his eyes. But he couldn't move. He couldn't even blink. He was staring helplessly into the red robot eyes. They were getting bigger and bigger. He was being dragged towards them. They were like the headlights of an oncoming train. Everything else in the room became blurred and dark. And there was a message for him.

Sam stopped trying to resist. He felt his body relax. He began to drift. It was a pleasant feeling. Nothing mattered any more.

Nothing at all.

Suddenly, *bang*, the bedroom door was flung open and someone stamped into the room.

'Mum says do you want any cake. And have you seen Max today . . . what are you doing?'

Sam distantly recognised the voice as Steph's. But it didn't mean anything to him. If she went away then the robot would be able to deliver the message. That was the only important thing.

'Wow! Is that the model robot? That looks amazing.' The voice paused for a second. 'Sam. What's going on?'

Sam saw a dark flickering shadow pass before his eyes. Steph was waving a hand in front of his face. He didn't blink. This disturbance was becoming annoying.

And then, just when he was losing himself in the robot's gaze again, the red lights suddenly disappeared. All at once the normal world returned, full of white sunlight and confusing colours. Sam blinked and gasped like a stranded fish. Steph had stepped between him and the robot, breaking the connection. Sam felt as if he'd been deeply asleep and had just been woken by a bucket of icy water. He was trembling all over.

Steph grabbed him by the arms. 'What's wrong with you?'

She helped him over to the bed. Sam sank down onto the heap of Bisky Bricks, completely disorientated. He looked around the bedroom, not really recognising anything. He could hear an angry humming noise coming from somewhere.

'Sam.' Steph sounded really worried. 'What's going on? Are you okay? You look awful.' She reached up to remove her alien helmet.

'No! Leave it on,' gasped Sam, suddenly remembering.

'I'll get Mum.' Steph stepped backwards, the alien helmet dangling from her hand, and then let out a piercing shriek. She leaped away from the desk rubbing her backside, twisting around, glaring. 'It bit me. Your model bit me. Really hard.'

'Keep away from it. Don't look at its eyes, put on your helmet,' said Sam, fumbling blindly with one hand under the bed. His fingers touched his own helmet. He yanked it out and shoved it on his head.

'Right through my shorts. There's a hole. Look. This thing's vicious.' There was a thump, a high, angry humming and a snapping noise. Sam peered through the little holes in his helmet visor. Steph was sucking an injured finger, glaring at the robot. 'It bit me again,' she said indignantly.

'Steph, don't look at it.'

But she was staring right into the robot's eyes. Sam lurched to his feet and shoved her aside.

'Wow!' she said. 'What kind of model is this? Its eyes are really weird. Kind of buzzy.'

'I know,' said Sam. 'Put your helmet back on.' He shoved her helmet onto her head.

He turned back to the robot, then reached down cautiously and picked up the empty saucepan from the floor.

'Stand back, Steph,' he said. 'I'm going to catch it.'

The robot's humming had become an angry, frustrated whine. It snapped its clutching-claw hands. Sam edged towards it. He turned the saucepan over and took another step. Its head swivelled to follow him. Sam lifted the saucepan.

There was a whining bark, a scuffle, and Moriarty came bounding into the bedroom. Sam caught his foot in the fallen chair, lost his balance and waved his arms around like a windmill. The saucepan banged into the side of Steph's helmet, knocking her over, then rolled away. Steph sprawled on the floor. Sam tripped over her and fell full length. The robot's wheels spun with a sudden whirring noise. It shot off the desk. Sam felt a thump as it bounced off the back of his helmet. He turned to see a shiny blur shoot through the open door and disappear.

He scrambled to his feet, still feeling trembly and weak, pushed Moriarty away, grabbed Steph by the arm and hauled her up.

'Are you okay?' he gasped.

She nodded. 'Are you?'

'Come on.' Sam picked up the saucepan. 'We've got to catch it. We've got to stop it. Before . . .' He didn't bother to finish his sentence.

He sprinted into the kitchen, clutching the saucepan, and halted, horrified. His heart gave one extra, enormous thump. He stumbled over his feet and nearly lost his balance. Steph banged into him from behind. Moriarty started barking.

Em was standing by the sink rinsing a face washer. Molly was sitting in her high chair surrounded by cake crumbs. And the robot was on the little table of the high chair only inches from Molly's face. Molly gurgled and reached out her hands.

Sam peered frantically around the room through the little holes in the helmet.

'What's going on?' said Em, turning from the sink, her costume flashing. 'Where've you been,

Sam? Everyone's gone home. You missed the cake.' She saw the robot. 'What's that? What's going on? Oh, and Mum wants to know if you've seen that Max today?'

'What?' said Sam. 'Watch out, don't look at it.' He lurched across the room and grabbed a wooden spoon from the draining board.

'That Max. From your class. He's gone missing, apparently. What are you doing? What is that thing?'

Sam thrust the spoon at the robot. The robot spun around with frightening speed. One clutching-claw hand shot out and snapped at the spoon. Sam felt it jerk as the robot chopped a claw-shaped piece out of the end. Splinters flew.

'Quick, grab Molly, Steph!' he shouted, shoving the robot with the spoon again. It teetered off-balance on the edge of the high chair, wheels spinning, arms circling in a blur. Steph leaped across and lifted Molly out of the chair.

'What's going on?' asked Em again.

'He's made this robot model,' explained Steph. 'You know, in the Bisky Bricks. It keeps trying to hypnotise people. It's amazing.'

'Is Molly okay?' Sam asked without moving his head, keeping the robot in sight.

'I think so,' said Steph. 'She looks a bit sleepy.'

Sam jabbed the spoon at the robot again, trying

to knock it off the high chair. Like a silver flash, a clutching claw shot out and snatched the spoon. Using the spoon as a lever, the robot spun around and with a whirr flipped itself into the air. Sam ducked and twisted as it flew over his head. The robot landed neatly, out of reach, on the table top behind him.

Em gasped.

'Wow,' Steph said. 'That was amazing.'

Moriarty started to bark even more loudly.

The robot stood poised like a cat about to pounce. Its head was swivelling around, red eyes glowing. Sam was sure it was looking for someone to hypnotise. It seemed very determined.

'You all go outside. Take Molly,' he said. 'It wants to hypnotise you. I'll try and catch it.'

'Do you know, Sam,' said Steph, 'some people say that praying mantises can do hypnotism when they're hunting. They hide, and when a bug comes along they move like this ... look, Sam, like this ...'

'Steph—' Just this once, why couldn't she do what he told her? Exasperated, he turned around. She was holding Molly with one arm, and the other was sticking up, presumably like a praying mantis hunting. 'Shut up, for one second, about insects. Take Molly outside. Now! It's dangerous. The robot is trying to ...'

He turned back to the table. He peered around frantically. The robot had disappeared.

'Where'd it go?' he gasped. 'Did you see where it went?'

'It's right down there,' said Em, pointing.

Sam turned. The robot was standing in the corner near the fridge, red eyes glowing.

'What's it doing?' asked Em.

'I just need to catch it, that's all. Don't look at it, or it will hypnotise you.'

'What?' demanded Em. 'Me? I don't think so.' She strode across to the robot, costume flashing, hands on her hips.

'No, Em. Don't look at it,' gasped Sam.

'Huh!' said Em, staring down at the glowing red eyes. 'I'd like to see it try to hypnotise *me*. Come on, little robot. Let's see what you've got.'

Sam gave an enormous sigh. What was it with sisters? Did they ever do what you told them? Arguing with Em was always pointless.

He edged towards the robot. There was a creak, and the floor seemed to tilt.

'I don't think it's working,' said Em scornfully.

Sam could see that the robot was confused. Instead of the steady red glow, it looked like it was blinking. Its head shifted, and then spun around.

'It's the costume,' said Em. 'Ha ha. I'm just too sparkly for it.'

She was right. From where it stood on the floor, the robot had to stare up the length of Em's dancing costume to meet her eyes. The mirrors and beads and twinkling lights were dazzling its hypnotising gaze. Its eyes blinked off and on again. Its head spun around and then spun back the other way. Its arms circled uncertainly.

'*Sparkle, sparkle, just the same*
As the sun's most sparkly rays.
Sparkle, sparkle, like a flame,
Glint and glisten, flash and blaze.'

The robot didn't seem to appreciate the 'Sparkle, sparkle' song. It lurched jerkily backwards.

Em approached, singing and swaying her hips. Her costume was dazzling. Sam couldn't look directly at it and the robot seemed to feel the same way. Its head jiggled from side to side and then spun right around again. Its arms circled, snapping. Its eyes blinked on and off.

Sam lifted the saucepan. Now was his chance. He leaped forward. At the same time, Moriarty made a lunge at the robot and Em did the dramatic jumping step that was part of her dance.

The whole kitchen lurched. There was a terrible grinding crash. And then the floor collapsed under them.

Chapter Thirteen

Sam dropped the saucepan and grabbed onto Em. She lost her balance and clutched at the table. It teetered, and fell over with a bang. Steph shrieked. Molly started to wail.

There was a horrible groaning creak as the kitchen tilted and collapsed. An enormous crash followed as the fridge toppled over. With a splintering noise, the floorboards snapped apart. Plates and cups slid off the bench and smashed. Sam scrabbled on the sloping floor, trying to get back to his feet. He looked over his shoulder.

Half of the kitchen had collapsed into a dark sandy hole. The fridge was lying at a strange angle, its door flapping open, milk and orange juice trickling out. Broken party streamers trailed limply. Green apples were rolling across the sloping floor and dropping one by one into the hole. The kitchen sink was tilting the other way. The cupboards on that side of the kitchen were splintered and broken, sloping drunkenly. Smashed plates and knives and forks were scattered everywhere. Water suddenly began squirting from a broken pipe.

Steph stood clutching Molly on the one section of floor that had survived. Her mouth was hanging open. She looked horrified. Molly was shrieking. Moriarty was barking. Sam and Em struggled to the only flat part of floor left and got gingerly to their feet.

Sam pulled off the alien helmet and looked around at the chaos. What would Mum and Dad say?

And where was the robot?

Mum was furious. Sam had never seen her so angry. She yelled and waved her arms about just like normal, but her eyes were scary-looking and her voice had a sharp edge, like a hacksaw. She was angry with them all. But mostly with Steph.

It was Steph's trench burrowing under the house that made the kitchen collapse.

Steph tried to explain about her insect survey and how the cold dark soil under the house had produced a different range of specimens than the soil from the back garden. Sam could have told her that this explanation would only make Mum more angry, and it did.

Steph started to cry. Tears trickled down her cheeks from under the visor of her alien helmet. Molly was still wailing and Em was pale. Moriarty cowered behind their legs, whining. Sam felt as if he had been caught up in a whirlwind.

Mum shouted while she turned off the water and the electricity at the mains, and after that she just stood and shouted.

Apparently Steph should have realised that the foundations of the house were necessary to hold the house up. And did she have any idea what this would cost to fix? And if any of them thought they'd ever have pocket money again in their lives they were mistaken, because the repairs would take it all until they were eighteen and even then it wouldn't be enough. Did they know how expensive kitchens were? And what their father would say, nobody could guess. There had never been such thoughtless, irresponsible, destructive children since the world began. What did they have between their ears anyway? Sawdust?

At last Mum paused for a breath. 'I always knew I should have gone on that cruise,' she said.

Sam started to relax. When Mum talked about going on that cruise, it was meant as a sort of joke. When Mum and Dad first met, Mum had been about to go on a holiday cruise with a bunch of friends from college. Instead of going, she had stayed behind and married Dad. Now, when things annoyed her, she would say she should have gone on that cruise, after all. Then she would laugh.

''m sorry,' mumbled Steph.

'Yes, well,' said Mum. She frowned at Steph, then glared around the wrecked kitchen. Her expression softened a little as she sighed and picked up Molly, who was wailing like a police siren. 'Well, don't do it again,' she said.

Sam felt like giggling but laughing right now would surely set Mum off again.

Mum picked up the phone. 'Oh, Sam,' she said. 'Have you seen Max today? He's missing.'

'Max? No. He's grounded, anyway.'

'Are you sure you haven't seen him? Do you know where he might be? His parents are frantic.'

Sam shook his head.

'Everyone's out searching. They've called the police,' said Mum, glaring at the phone. She hung up and tried again. 'Oh, for goodness sake. On top of everything else.' She picked up the phone cord and saw that it had been torn out of the wall when the kitchen collapsed. She slammed down the receiver.

'Right. That's it,' she snapped. 'I'm going to take Molly and find a phone that works. I'll try and get someone out to fix this disaster. You three. Outside. Touch nothing. I mean it. Nothing.' She glanced uncertainly around the kitchen. 'Well, I wouldn't think you could do any more damage, but keep out of the house. Just try not to destroy anything else. Em, you're in charge. I won't be too long. And Sam, try to think where Max might be. Okay?'

As they followed Mum out to the front garden, Em cautiously asked, 'Where's Dad?'

'He went off with Uncle Andy,' said Mum, locking the front door. 'Heaven knows what he'll say when he sees this.' She shook her head and gave another exasperated sigh. 'Stay right there,' she said as she got into the car. 'Keep out of trouble.'

Mum drove away. Even the car sounded angry. Sam caught Em's eye, and they both broke into sudden, nervous laughter. Even Steph was half laughing through her tears.

'At least she didn't find out about the robot,' Sam gasped. 'She wouldn't have liked that.'

'Where did it go?' asked Em.

'It must have fallen in the hole. I hope it's okay.'

'Yes, of course. The kitchen's smashed to bits and we've no pocket money ever again, but as long as your stupid robot's okay . . .'

'Ha ha. There's cake left, anyway.'

There was a biggish wedge of birthday cake left on the table in the front garden. Em cut it into three fat pieces. Sam broke his piece in two and gave half to Moriarty. They flopped down on the grass. Sam found a half-full bottle of fizzy drink and they passed it between them. The cake was comforting. Steph stopped crying, apart from an occasional sniff. Sam realised he had been shaking. He patted Moriarty's head and felt himself relax.

'I wonder where that Max has got to. I hope he's okay,' said Em.

'He was grounded,' said Sam. 'He was making a robot, too. He'd nearly finished. It smashed all this stuff in their house and his mum . . .' He stopped. His heart gave a lurch.

'His mum what?' asked Em.

Sam didn't answer. He was thinking about when he'd talked to Max on the phone. Max said he had nearly finished his robot and he'd sounded really weird. Not like himself at all.

'He said he was going to follow it . . .' Sam said.

'What?'

'Max. He said he was going to follow the robot. It must have hypnotised him. He must have finished it, and then he must have followed it.'

'Why? Where?'

Sam shrugged. 'I don't know. I bet that's what happened, though.'

Steph said, 'Then, to find Max . . .'

Sam finished her thought. 'I should let my robot hypnotise me. Yes, of course.' He got to his feet. 'Then it will lead me to wherever Max is.'

'Why would it?' asked Em. 'It might lead you anywhere. Sam, what are you doing?'

Sam tried the front door. Locked. 'Round the back!' he said urgently.

In the back garden they could see how the kitchen had collapsed into Steph's trench. On either side, part of the house was sloping into a dark hole. When he got onto his hands and knees Sam could see right into the house. Bits of the ruined kitchen and parts of cupboards were sitting at strange angles in a few inches of muddy water. Was the robot under there somewhere?

He fetched the rake from the shed and fished under the house with it.

'Careful, Sam,' said Em. 'Don't go underneath. It might fall on you.'

Moriarty started to bark anxiously.

'I can see it,' said Sam. 'It's behind the fridge.'

The shiny white surface of the fridge was reflecting a glowing red light. Sam clambered down into the trench. Mud came up over his runners and soaked into his socks. He poked the rake further under the fridge.

'I think it's stuck,' he said. 'Pass me the spade.'

Steph passed it to him. He thrust it under the

fridge and scraped out some mud. The house gave a groaning creak. Sam froze. Would it collapse even further?

Nothing happened.

Cautiously, he stuck the spade under the fridge again. *Snap!* He jumped. Steph gave a nervous little scream. There was a wet, whirring sound and the robot shot out from under the fridge spraying water from its spinning wheels. It was splattered with mud, but parts of it were still gleaming silver and its red eyes were glowing. It zoomed towards Sam.

He dropped the spade and tried to climb out of the trench. The edges were crumbly and soft. *Snap, snap.* The robot was attacking his ankles.

'Owww! Help!'

Steph and Em grabbed one arm each and hauled him out.

They looked down at the robot. It was zooming around the bottom of the trench. It seemed to be looking for a way out. It tried to climb up the steep crumbling side but fell back.

Sam patted Moriarty. 'It's okay, dog,' he said. 'You can stop barking. We're all safe.'

'So what are you going to do?' asked Em.

'I'm going to let it hypnotise me,' said Sam. 'And you two can follow me and see where it goes. Then we'll find Max. Steph, you wear your helmet, so you'll be safe from the robot. Em, you can wear mine if you want.'

'I don't need a helmet,' said Em. 'I've got my costume. But, Sam, I don't know. Maybe we should wait for Mum.'

'She might be ages,' said Sam. 'And Max might be, I don't know, in danger. We should do this straight away.' He wanted to do it before he lost his nerve.

'Well . . .' said Em.

'Okay, then. Hang on to Moriarty.' Sam swallowed. 'Ready?'

They nodded—Steph firmly, Em uncertainly. Steph gripped Moriarty's collar.

Sam lowered himself back into the trench. The robot's head swivelled to follow him. Its red eyes seemed to glow more brightly. Sam crouched in the mud, then lifted his gaze and looked fully into the glowing red stare.

Just like before, the red eyes seemed to draw him closer. His head swam. The whole world was made up of red light. And there was a message.

Sam felt himself relax. Nothing mattered any more, nothing but the message.

Chapter Fourteen

It was as if the robot delivered the message right into Sam's brain. It was very clear and very simple. He understood exactly what he had to do.

Follow.

Sam had no further worries or doubts. He didn't even have to look in the robot's eyes any more because now his whole head was full of red light. He felt like he was floating. All he needed to do was to follow the robot. He would follow wherever it went.

He calmly reached out and picked it up. He knew it wouldn't attack him. Then he climbed out of the trench and set the robot back on the ground.

Its wheels whirred and it set off across the garden.

Sam followed. He felt relaxed and sure. The robot led him around the house, across the front garden and out into the street.

Suddenly there was a growl and a grey blur. A big hairy dog was snarling at the robot and trying to bite it. How annoying. There was a *snap*, and then a yelp. The dog jumped back.

'Sam, Sam, wait for us. Stop it, Moriarty.'

He could hear voices, but he didn't bother to listen. There were running footsteps, and someone grabbed the dog by its collar and dragged it away. He saw a strange figure, shortish and wearing a silver helmet with waving antennae. He felt like he should remember who this was, but right at the moment it didn't seem important.

'Hang on, Sam,' said the figure. 'We're just finding a lead for Moriarty. Em's looking in the shed.'

Sam turned and started walking again. The short silver-headed person grabbed at his arm. 'Sam. Wait a second.'

'A second,' he said.

'Or two or three. Em's looking for some rope.'

Sam was annoyed by the interruption. 'Follow,' he explained, loudly and firmly, trying to pull away and keep walking. Fingers dug into his arm. The robot was a little way in front. Its head swivelled as it looked back at them. Then, with a whirr, it turned a tight circle and zoomed towards them, snapping its claw hands.

Snap, snap, snap.

It went straight for the ankles of the arm-grabbing person, making it shriek and hop from foot to foot.

'Ouch!' it yelled.

The dog started to bark. The person let go of Sam's arm and leaped away from the attacking robot, keeping hold of the barking dog. The robot immediately stopped snapping, turned, and headed off down the footpath.

Good, thought Sam and followed.

They were halfway along the foreshore when three figures came running up behind him, making a lot of annoying and distracting noise.

'You look really weird.' A taller person, with an outfit so sparkling and dazzling that it made him blink, came up beside him and looked into his face. 'Are you okay?'

'Okay,' he said. This person looked familiar as well, but Sam couldn't remember who it was. Someone he'd met once? Not to worry. It wasn't important.

'Where's it going, do you think? Oh, shut up, you stupid dog.' She was hanging tightly onto a piece of rope attached to the dog. It was still barking loudly, pulling on the rope, snarling at the robot.

The little robot zoomed along the foreshore and Sam quickened his pace. Maybe these irritating people would be left behind.

But they kept up, talking to each other all the way. They didn't seem to shut up even for a second. Sam tried not to listen. The only thing that mattered was to follow the robot. Several other people on the foreshore and on the beach stared at them as they passed. Sam noticed them looking, but he didn't care. Although he could see people pointing, and hear them talking and laughing, it wasn't important.

'Sam, Sam,' said the shorter person as the road started to climb. 'It's going to Magic Mart, I think. It's taking us to Magic Mart.'

'Magic Mart,' said Sam. He'd heard that name before. 'Magic Mart,' he repeated. Of course! He recognised the tall brick building. *Magic Mart*, he read, spelled out above the door in large red letters.

It looked welcoming.

The robot zoomed in through the main doors. Sam followed. After the bright sunshine, it was dim and dark inside. He could hear the two people arguing as they tied the dog's rope to a pole outside. The sound of the dog's frantic barking receded, and now he could hear other voices and some kind of wailing music. The first thing he saw was a huge pile of boxes, each with a picture of a robot on it. *Bisky Bricks*, he thought.

He felt a sharp nip on his ankle and looked down to see the robot glaring up at him.

'Follow,' Sam said. He turned away from the Bisky Bricks and followed his own robot down an aisle, around a corner, down another aisle, past pyramids of brightly coloured cans and teetering piles of cereal boxes.

The two annoying people seemed to be dropping behind. He could hear their voices arguing a long way off. The robot zoomed past a big display of dog food and banged into a door. Sam reached out and turned the handle. He pulled the door open and the robot shot through. Sam followed.

The robot skidded down a flight of stairs—*bang, bang, bang*—zoomed around a small landing and shot down another flight. Sam went after it. He could see a strange greenish light glowing from down below, and he could hear voices, but he felt no curiosity.

Follow, he thought.

At the bottom of the stairs was a storeroom. There was a pile of dusty cardboard boxes against one wall, and an enormous heap of rocks and gravel in the middle of the floor. A bunch of shovels and pickaxes were stacked up against the wall. The robot skirted the rocks and crossed the room to a metal door that led into a rough, rocky tunnel lit by a green light.

A figure stepped through the doorway. The robot slowed and Sam stopped. He looked at the man. He had to squint because the man was silhouetted against the green glow, but Sam could see he had a dark beard and was wearing a furry black hat.

'Ah! Good,' said the man in a deep soft voice. 'Another one. Excellent.' He stepped towards Sam and pulled something from his pocket. It looked like a mobile phone, except that it had a bright red light on the top of it. As he spoke into it the light glowed even more brightly. 'Come. Here is another. Take his arms. Do not let go.'

Two more figures appeared. One was tall and thin and looked familiar, but Sam couldn't think who it was. Someone he knew from somewhere?

The two men grabbed Sam's arms. He didn't mind. He walked calmly through the doorway and along the tunnel, following the robot.

And then, finally, the robot stopped. Its red eyes blinked off. The word *Follow*, which had been echoing inside Sam's head, began to dissolve like a marshmallow in a cup of hot chocolate.

The dizzying red light that been surrounding his brain faded away.

And then, all at once, the normal world flooded back.

Em and Steph, he thought. *Mum. Dad. Molly. Moriarty.* Sam remembered the kitchen collapsing. He remembered Molly's birthday party. He remembered the strange lights in the sky. And he remembered why he was here. Max was missing, and they'd come to find him.

Suddenly Sam was properly back inside himself. He blinked and looked around. The short tunnel had opened into a cave. The walls and floor were rock and the ceiling arched overhead. He realised he was being held tightly by both arms.

'Hey!' he yelled, struggling furiously. 'Hey! Let me go!' He twisted around. On one side was a Magic Mart teenager with a red uniform and a vacant-looking face. On the other side ... Sam felt his heart give a lurch. 'Uncle Andy—'

Uncle Andy looked down at Sam with no expression at all. His face was eerie in the green light. But calm. Blank. Sam could see no recognition.

'Uncle Andy. It's me. Sam,' he gasped.

'Sam,' agreed Uncle Andy. His face didn't change. His eyes didn't focus.

Sam felt suddenly weak and frightened.

The bearded man reached down his leather-gloved hand to pick up the robot. It immediately came back to life and twirled out of his reach, snapping its claws. The man said something under his breath and tried again.

The robot dashed towards him, darted between his legs, snapping, and zipped away. It turned a somersault, wheels whizzing loudly, then shot back towards the man.

It looked like the robot wanted to play.

The man muttered a foreign word. He sounded very annoyed. He tried to catch the robot again, but it flipped into the air, over his grasping hand, and spun away from him. The man crouched, and this time he kept quite still until the robot approached, snapping and humming, and then he suddenly snatched it up in both hands. It twisted and snapped at his gloves, but he held onto it firmly.

'You will go in my case with the other one,' he said.

Then, transferring the snapping robot carefully to one hand, he pulled the phone out of his pocket, pressed a button, and said, 'Leave him. Go.'

Uncle Andy and the Magic Mart teenager let go of Sam's arms and turned away so quickly that Sam lost his balance and fell over. He struggled back to his feet, still feeling dizzy and weak.

'Hey, Uncle Andy!' he called, staggering after the two men.

But Uncle Andy and the teenager had already gone. The bearded man gave one glance back at Sam and left as well. Sam dashed along the tunnel and flung himself at the door just as it clanged shut. He grabbed the handle and rattled it. His heart sank as he heard the key turn in the lock.

'Uncle Andy,' he yelled. 'Let me out.'

But there was no answer. The door was firmly shut. Sam kicked it, and only managed to hurt his foot. He yelled and rattled the handle again. But it was pointless. He was locked in. And he was alone.

He turned his back to the door and looked around the cave. Perhaps there was another way out. He looked up to where the green light was coming from.

'What . . .' he began.

Overhead a bright light was gleaming through what looked like a forest of enormous dangling pillows. The pillows were wrapped in thick shiny threads, and each one was hanging from the rocky ceiling by a twisted rope. Several of the pillows were slowly revolving. There were maybe thirty of them, and they pulsed with glowing green light.

Then Sam felt his stomach turn over. Something had moved. One of the pillows was squirming. It looked, all at once, not like a pillow but an enormous green maggot wrapped up like a parcel.

And then Sam realised what they were. He'd seen things like this often enough. Steph sometimes found them and let them hatch on the windowsill of her room. But the ones that Steph collected were smaller than a finger. And they usually hatched out into butterflies. So what would hatch out of cocoons that were this big? Fear clutched at Sam's heart and he felt sick.

He tiptoed under the enormous dangling maggots and looked up to the bright light that shone in the ceiling. It was in fact a big hole, high in the wall, through which Sam saw a patch of sunny blue sky. He realised that he was in a cave in the cliff face below Magic Mart. He could hear the waves, and seagulls calling. Someone must have dug a short tunnel connecting the Magic Mart basement with this cave. But why?

Suddenly a brilliant orange light appeared, flying in a bright, curving path across the patch of blue sky. Sam's heart gave a jump. The light slowed and seemed to pause. For a moment Sam thought it had stopped moving. But as he watched he saw it was getting bigger and brighter.

His mouth fell open as he suddenly realised that it was moving really fast, and that it was heading his way.

Chapter Fifteen

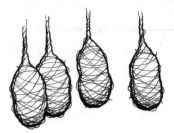

Sam froze for a second, staring up at the light in the sky. Then he sprinted back to the door and frantically twisted the handle. He thumped the door, yelling. He flung his full weight against it. Nothing happened, except that now his shoulder hurt.

He rushed back to look out at the sky. The orange light was much larger and brighter than before. It was travelling frighteningly fast. Whatever it was, it would arrive within seconds. Sam looked desperately around the cave for somewhere to hide. The tunnel was too short; there was nowhere to hide there. The walls were rocky and uneven. Maybe there was an overhang or a tiny recess somewhere?

There was a smallish loose boulder lying in a corner of the cave. It was the only possible hiding place. Sam scrambled across the cave and ducked behind it.

He found himself staring into Max's frightened eyes.

Sam gasped. The boulder was Max.

Max was wrapped up like a mummy in a thick covering of sticky threads with only his eyes and his nose showing. He looked like an enormous sticky ball of pale brown wool.

Sam reached out and pulled some of the threads away from Max's mouth. They were stretchy and sticky, like spider web, but much stronger. Sam managed to pull enough away for Max to take a shuddering breath. He gulped, spat some sticky threads out of his braces, and coughed.

'Sam,' he wheezed.

'What?'

'Look out!' gasped Max.

Sam turned and felt every muscle in his body freeze in terror.

The mysterious orange light had arrived.

Sam had never seen anything like it. It was enormous. And it shone so brightly that Sam could hardly look at it. For a moment it hovered outside, shining in through the hole like a small sun. Then a spindly leg felt its way into the cave. Another limb followed, and another, and then the whole creature pulled itself inside. Sam's stomach lurched. The thing's jointed legs were impossibly long and skinny, and it seemed to have at least eight of them. It was like an armour-plated spider. Its body was like a flash of orange light. It was so dazzling that Sam had to squint.

It filled the cave. Its legs easily reached to the walls and it brushed against the hanging cocoons and made them swing from side to side.

Sam's mouth was so dry he couldn't swallow. He shrank behind the sticky ball that was Max and hoped desperately that the thing wouldn't see him. He glanced at Max, but Max had his eyes tightly shut and his whole face was screwed up.

The spider seemed to be checking the cocoons one by one. It was making a high-pitched, chattering noise. One of its legs was so close to Sam that he could have reached out and touched it. He stared in terrified fascination. What was it made of? It looked like some kind of glowing metal.

At last the spider finished with the cocoons and spun around with a swift sweeping motion. It reached out one leg and rolled Max aside. Sam was exposed. He was too terrified to do anything but stare stupidly up at it. He could see lots of blobby things, which might have been eyes, as well as snipping jaw things. He was so frightened he felt he might be sick.

The creature reached for Sam. He shut his eyes tightly as he felt himself being grabbed by hard, strong, claw-like pincers. They were surprisingly cold. Then he was lifted up. The last thing he heard was a high-pitched chattering, and a *snip, snip* noise, as if it was snapping its jaws. His last thought was, *it's going to eat me.* And then, for the first time in his life, he fainted.

Sam woke up, opened his eyes and stared blankly. At first he couldn't think where he was. He tried to lift up a hand, but it seemed to be stuck to his side. He tried the other hand. He couldn't even wriggle his fingers.

Slowly his brain started to wake up. Then he remembered the glowing spider. He tried to yell, but he couldn't open his mouth; he couldn't even turn his head. With a horrible sinking feeling, he squinted downwards.

He was wrapped up like Max. Like a parcel. Wrapped around with strong sticky threads. Only his eyes and his nose were free. He was lying on his back on the rocky floor, as round as an enormous fat potato. He breathed in as deeply as he could through his nose and tried not to panic.

At least he was alive, he thought. At least the spider thing hadn't eaten him. That was something.

He blinked his eyes. The spider had gone. The

green cocoons were still dangling from the roof and the sunshine was shining through the hole in the cave. But, mostly, all he could see was the curved edge of another wrapped-up parcel. Was it Max?

'Sam? Sam?' The voice came from the other parcel.

Sam made a sort of muffled grunting noise.

'You're awake!' said Max. 'Are you okay? You've been asleep for ages. I'm so happy you're here.'

Sam made a not very agreeing noise.

'It was really horrible by myself. It's much better now you're here,' Max went on. 'Do you know what's happening? Do you know what that thing is? What do you think it's going to do to us? Something awful, probably.' After a pause, he added, 'I was grounded, you know. But I sneaked out and got enough of those Bisky Bricks to finish the robot. All I could think of was following it. That's all I wanted. I followed it here.' He stopped again, and then said, 'Mum and Dad are going to kill me for this.'

Sam grunted again. Before Max could continue, a key turned in the lock and the door clanged open. The man with the beard and the furry hat walked into the cave and came over to them.

'Very good,' he said, in his soft low voice. 'Everything is working extremely well.'

Sam glared at him, but it was hard to look tough and threatening when he was lying on the ground wrapped up like a sticky bundle.

Max took a shaky breath and said, 'What's going on? What was that thing? Who are you? What are you going to do with us?'

The man looked surprised. 'To do with you? Nothing.' He rubbed his hands together and went on. 'I am Valya Vlastov. Senior Professor Vlastov. I am an astro-entomologist. I arranged for you to come here, to this nest. I designed little robots to bring you. Modified, perhaps I should say. And I programmed the robot with one word only: "Follow". Genius, do you not think? Such technology. I should not have used toys, of course, no. That is clear, now. They behave very foolishly. So now they have brought you here, I must take them apart again, into tiny pieces. That way there is less trouble. And the Bisky Bricks. Kelp biscuits. No child can resist them, of course, no. My mother's recipe, God rest her soul. When I was a little boy, I would so look forward to my mother's cooking. Blood sausage, fermented cabbage, and then kelp biscuits for a real treat. These biscuits, though, have a little added something. To make the robot's work easier.'

Sam remembered the times he'd found himself staring blankly at bright lights over the last few days. Eating all those Bisky Bricks had made him easier to hypnotise.

'This way, there will be fresh meat coming here every day or two,' the professor went on. He turned away and looked up at the hanging cocoons. 'For when the young ones hatch.'

Sam suddenly felt icy deep down in the pit of his stomach. He remembered Steph's disgusting story about the wasp that paralysed a caterpillar and left it alive to be eaten by the baby wasps when they hatched. He realised that he and Max were like that caterpillar. When the giant green maggots hatched, they wouldn't have to go far to find their first breakfast.

'What was that thing?' asked Max, his voice trembling.

'Aha,' said Professor Vlastov, rubbing his gloved hands together again. 'A genuine alien. A space insect. When I started talking about space insects, they said I was mad. Mad!' He gave a mad-sounding laugh that made Sam's blood feel like iced water. 'But I find nests so I can breed them. Soon they will be everywhere. Ha ha ha! Then we shall see who's mad! Soon the whole world will know of my space insects. Mad? They won't be calling me mad, then. Of course, no. They will be begging me to return. I am the world expert. I have all the knowledge.'

'Please let us go,' quavered Max.

'Oh, no, no,' said Professor Vlastov in his reasonable voice. 'I could not do that. Of course, no. You are part of my plan. They thought, when they closed my beautiful laboratory, that my work would end. They said I could not continue. But there will soon be space insects all over the world, and I will be the only expert. Astro-entomology is more important than you two little boys. There are millions of people in the world. You are quite expendable.'

He had his back to them as he gazed up at the dangling cocoons. 'They are nearly ready to hatch,' he said. 'She will be visiting more often. I must find more meat.'

A sudden sparkle of light caught Sam's eye. He rolled his eyes and looked across to the tunnel entrance. Behind Max, he could see Em and Steph creeping into the cave looking determined and brave. Steph had taken off her alien helmet and was holding a plastic cricket bat. Em had a rake.

Sam held his breath. *Don't turn around*, he thought desperately.

Suddenly Uncle Andy was in the doorway. 'Intruders,' he called.

Professor Vlastov swung around and saw Em and Steph. Em lifted the rake and bashed

Professor Vlastov hard with it. The professor howled and lurched out of Sam's view, clutching his nose. There were more thumps and scuffling sounds. Someone yelled. Sam saw Steph jab the cricket bat forcefully into Uncle Andy's stomach and, when he bent double, give him a wallop on his head.

For a moment it looked like Steph and Em might actually get the better of the two men, but then the professor gabbled some instruction into his phone and two Magic Mart teenagers came running. In a few more moments Em and Steph had been disarmed and were held tightly with their arms pinned behind their backs.

Professor Vlastov had blood trickling from his nose, but his expression was quite calm. He pressed another button on his phone and spoke into it. 'Come in here,' he said quietly.

Em and Steph, who had been struggling furiously, suddenly stopped and stared open-mouthed down the tunnel. From where he was lying, Sam couldn't see what they were looking at.

'Hold them here,' said Professor Vlastov into the phone. 'Don't let them go. Watch them.' He dabbed at his bleeding nose with a handkerchief.

And then, in a day of terrible surprises, Sam received another shock. Someone had come into the cave. Steph and Em looked even more astonished . . . and then the man came into view. His face was blank and expressionless like Uncle Andy's, but even more familiar.

It was Dad.

Chapter Sixteen

The men and the Magic Mart teenagers had left. The door had clanged shut. Em and Steph had thumped on it. They had shouted and argued and pleaded. But there was no response.

Em kicked the door and said a string of really rude words. Steph looked like she was going to cry. Em gave the door one last kick and then trailed over to where Sam and Max were lying like two enormous sticky pillows. Steph stood with her back to them, sniffing and looking up at the dangling cocoons.

'Oh no. What's going to happen to us?' Max was groaning. 'We're all going to be eaten. Oh no, oh no!'

Sam grunted and rolled his eyes around.

'What?' said Em crossly. 'What happened to you two? What's going on here?' She knelt down and pulled the sticky threads away from Sam's face. '*Eugh*,' she said, rubbing her hands together.

'What is this stuff? I don't want to get it on my costume. Oh, stop moaning, Max.'

'Unwrap me, too,' Max said. 'We need to get out of here.'

Sam spluttered and coughed. He spat sticky threads out of his teeth. He took a deep breath in through his mouth.

'Steph, come and give me a hand with this,' said Em. 'Sam, what's with Dad? And Uncle Andy? They didn't recognise us at all. That was so creepy. And why're you wrapped up like this? What are those weird things up there? And who's that man?'

'Unwrap me, too, Em,' repeated Max. 'I've been here longer than Sam. It's horrible in here. I had to pee, before.'

'Yuck, Max,' said Em. She started to unwind the threads from Sam's head. They tangled stickily around her hands and arms. 'Oh, *euugh*,' she said. 'This is disgusting.' She shuddered and tried to scrape the threads off her hands. 'This stuff is way too sticky. We need scissors or something. So, what's going on, Sam?'

'Well, that man . . .' started Sam.

'We're going to be eaten by aliens,' said Max. Then he went back to moaning under his breath, saying, 'Oh no, oh no,' again and again.

'Yeah. Well, that man, he's a nut,' said Sam. He

144

tried to ignore Max. He already felt quite scared enough. 'I mean, he made the robots so that we'd follow them here, and he's hypnotised Dad and Uncle Andy and those Magic Mart teenagers so they do what he says . . .' He stopped to think for a second, '. . . when he talks into that little phone with the light on. That's how he controls them. We should try and get hold of that phone, if we can. Anyway, there's this . . . well, it's like a really gigantic orange glowing spider. That's the weird light people have been seeing in the sky. Every time it flies here or flies away, people think it's a comet or a flying saucer. It's an alien. It fills the whole cave. It wrapped us up. Those things up there are its babies.'

Steph was staring at the cocoons. 'I think they're about to hatch.' She pointed. 'That one there. It's starting to glow, sort of orange coloured. It's starting to break open, I think.'

Sam felt sick. He struggled to move, but he was still pinned tightly with sticky threads. It was taking ages for Em to unwrap him. His head wasn't even free yet. He groaned. 'When they hatch they're going to eat us up. Max and me. And maybe you two, as well. We're their first meal. We've got to get out of here.'

'How can we?' Steph was looking out at the sky. 'We can't climb up there. It's way too high.

And even if we did, we'd just be out on the cliff face. We wouldn't be able to get away.'

'We'll have to make a run for it,' said Em. 'Next time someone comes in. I'll distract them and, Steph, you run for help. As fast as you can.'

It sounded risky.

Suddenly Steph said, 'What's that?'

She was pointing to the hole in the wall and out at the sky. Sam couldn't see from where he was lying, but he could guess what it was.

Em went over to Steph, and looked too. She gasped.

'What is it?' asked Sam, trying to keep his voice calm.

'A light in the sky,' said Em.

'It's getting bigger,' said Steph.

'Oh no,' said Max.

The alien was coming back. Sam struggled to escape from the sticky parcel. His head and neck were partly free, but he still couldn't move his arms. Em rushed to the door and kicked it again and again. Steph stood as if frozen and stared out at the sky.

'Why's it coming back so soon?' Sam muttered to himself, straining against the layers of sticky threads.

'It must be because her babies are hatching,' Steph said. 'She'll be coming much more often to check up on them. Insects can be really good parents, you know.'

'Steph,' yelled Sam. 'It's not coming for a little social visit. It's going to wrap you up and feed you to those great big maggots up there. Try to think of a way out of this.'

'Well, I'm just saying,' said Steph.

Sam gave a groaning, desperate sigh and tried to think. What could they do? There was nowhere to hide. There was no escape. They were trapped. He could see the orange glow now, as the alien flew closer and closer. It was as if the rising sun was shining into the cave, an orange beam slanting across the floor.

And then it was there, just outside.

Em and Steph screamed. They dashed from wall to wall and then ducked behind Sam and Max.

One long, glowing alien leg felt its way inside the hole. Then another. They all watched, dumbstruck and horrified, as the creature pulled itself inside. To Sam, it seemed even bigger than before. The huge body glowed above them like a small sun, and the eight skinny jointed legs filled the cave. There was a high-pitched, chattering noise.

Sam felt a horrible sense of inevitability as he watched the alien check the dangling cocoons. A couple of them were now glowing faintly, and it spent more time on these, chattering and running its legs along the outside of them.

Minutes passed. Sam held his breath. No one moved. Then the giant spider turned and, with one leg, rolled first Max and then Sam across the floor of the cave.

The world spun around. Sam bumped into something and stopped rolling, but he was now lying face down and he couldn't see anything but floor. He tried to twist his head around. Then Em screamed. There was more chattering from the alien, followed by the *snip, snip* noise. This went on for a bit. Suddenly he felt a slight bump. A voice whispered in his ear.

'It's me. Em. It's wrapping up Steph. I don't know if it's seen me. I'll just . . .' She broke off with a gasp. 'Oh no.'

There was a series of bumps and thumps and more chattering. With an enormous effort, using his head and neck like a lever, Sam rocked himself onto his side so he could see what was happening.

Steph had been wrapped up like a parcel and now lay silent and helpless on the other side of the cave. But Em was running. She ducked and weaved and swayed away from the grasping legs of the spider.

Then suddenly she reached around and

switched on the twinkling lights of her costume. The alien jerked back, chattering. Sam couldn't believe it. It was actually backing away.

Em danced forward.

Sam had never seen anything so brave in his life.

'*Sparkle, sparkle, everyone,*
Sparkle, sparkle, shine so bright,
Sparkle like the morning sun,
Sparkle like the stars at night.'

'Your sister's amazing,' whispered Max.

'I know,' said Sam.

The alien suddenly lunged at Em, but Em stood her ground. She looked bravely up at the spider and kept dancing. When she began the next verse of the 'Sparkle' song, her voice only trembled a bit. For a second, it looked like the alien spider would leave her alone. Sam started to feel hopeful.

But then, all of a sudden, it grabbed her.

Em screamed as she was lifted off her feet. She kicked and struggled and yelled. *Snip, snip.* The alien snapped its jaws and a thread shot out from them. Holding Em between two legs, it spun her around and around, wrapping her up. At first the sparkly lights on her costume were still visible, flashing brightly through the layers of thread, but soon they dimmed, and then they were gone altogether. Em's shouts became muffled.

It happened very fast. In just a few moments she was wrapped up tightly, silent and still.

Thump. The alien dropped Em next to Steph and then, with quick flicks of its legs, rolled all four of them together into one corner of the cave. Sam watched the world spin around until he bumped into Max and came to rest.

He felt his heart sink even further. There was nothing left for them to do but wait to be eaten, one by one, as the baby aliens hatched out of their cocoons.

As the spider climbed awkwardly out through the hole and launched itself into the sky, Sam noticed, without much surprise, that one of the cocoons was, in fact, starting to hatch. A crack had opened along one side, and an orange glow was shining out. As he watched, a spindly leg unfolded itself from inside the cocoon and waved uncertainly.

This is the end, Sam thought.

Chapter Seventeen

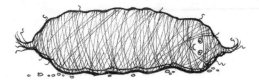

Sam lay there, helpless, and watched a second jointed leg poke itself out of the hatching cocoon. He thought about Mum. She wouldn't be happy to hear they'd all been eaten up by aliens. A despairing, cold feeling welled up in his throat and his eyes began to sting.

He could hear Em making muffled grunting noises. Steph was sniffing.

'Don't worry, Steph. We'll be okay,' he said, trying to keep his voice steady and sound like he meant it.

He took a deep breath. How would they get out of this? He couldn't move, of course, but he could still think and he could still talk. And so could Max.

It's up to me, he thought. *It's up to me and Max.*

'Sam, what are we going to do?' quavered Max. 'It's hatching. It's going to eat us. Oh no, oh no!' He sounded really frightened.

'We'll just have to think of something,' said Sam. 'We'll be okay. We'll get out of this.'

A key turned in the lock.

'Ah. Excellent,' said Professor Vlastov, stepping briskly into the cave. He smiled up at the hatching cocoon, his teeth gleaming. Three long orange legs had now emerged and were waving in the air. He turned to the four wrapped-up parcels on the floor. 'Plenty of fresh meat, all ready.' He rubbed his hands together.

Sam cleared his throat. 'Um. Professor Vlastov . . .' he began.

'*Senior* Professor Vlastov.'

'Oh, sorry. Senior Professor Vlastov,' said Sam. *Great start*, he thought. He took a breath. 'Please, can you let us go? Please? Don't leave us here.'

'Please,' Max added, his voice shaking.

Em and Steph made muffled, agreeing noises.

Professor Vlastov frowned. 'No, no. Of course no,' he said in his reasonable, soft voice. 'When the young one is hatched, it is very hungry. Very hungry. For this nest, my robots must bring plenty of meat. In other places I use ten, twenty children.'

Sam gulped. 'Other places?'

Professor Vlastov waved a hand in an irritable way. 'I go to wherever there is a nest. People see flying saucers, strange lights in the sky, and at once I know. All over the world. In many different places. Often there is trouble when I try to snatch fresh meat in the streets, so this time I bring my Bisky Bricks and my little robots. This is much more clever, the robots bring the fresh meat straight to the nest. But it is the same everywhere. The nest is always in a cave near the sea. Here it is easy. I see the television reports of the strange lights. I find the nest, here next to this store. I program the store manager and the workers to dig this small tunnel from the basement, so I can reach the nest. Then I teach them to say, "There is nothing in the basement. There is no man. There are no lights in the sky". It is the same everywhere. Although,' he frowned, 'in other places, the meat does not talk so much. Of course, no.'

'Um, Prof—I mean, *Senior* Professor Vlastov—' started Sam.

'No. No. Enough,' said the professor. He pulled the little phone out of his pocket. The red light blinked on. He pressed a couple of buttons and spoke into it. 'Come in here.'

After a moment, Dad and Uncle Andy walked into the cave and stood side by side, their faces blank, arms hanging. Professor Vlastov pressed a button and spoke into the phone again. 'Stay here. Watch that,' he pointed up at the cocoon.

'Let me know when it hatches. Don't talk to the meat.' He pressed another button, and said, 'You, come with me.'

He turned and left without a backwards glance. Uncle Andy followed him. Dad turned his blank face towards the cocoon and stared unblinking at it.

Sam remembered how he himself had felt when he was hypnotised. It had been a weird feeling. He'd not recognised anyone, not even Moriarty.

'Dad?' he tried, 'it's Sam. Sam and Em and Steph. Dad? Dad?'

Nothing. Not even a flicker of recognition.

Sam realised it was up to him and that this was his only chance. There had to be some way of getting through to Dad. Surely. When Sam had been hypnotised he hadn't recognised people, but he'd recognised a few things. Magic Mart. The Bisky Bricks boxes.

Maybe Dad would remember things too. What things did Dad love the most? That was easy. Fridges.

'Um. Hey, Dad,' Sam said. 'How about that new Freezomatic 5000? Top of the range.'

Nothing.

'With that twin cooling system,' said Sam. 'And the SuperFresh vegetable compartment.'

Dad didn't even blink.

Sam tried again. 'Hey, Dad, I bet you're looking forward to the new model Cool King. With the Multi-freeze ice feature. Imagine that sitting in the showroom. All shiny and white and excellent.'

Dad blinked.

Max gasped and Em and Steph made muffled, encouraging noises.

'Right.' Sam racked his brains, trying to remember all the fridge facts he'd ever heard. 'Okay,' he said. 'Well, Dad, what about those Icemasters? They're pretty good, with the triple evaporator system. And they've got the ice dispenser right there in the door. What do you think about them?'

Dad turned his head. His vacant gaze fixed briefly on Sam then turned back to the cocoon, which now had about six legs waving in the air. Sam guessed they had maybe two minutes before the alien hatched. What else could he say about fridges? Then he remembered the kitchen. Nothing, he was sure, would be more important to Dad than the lovely new fridge that had fallen into the trench.

'Hey, guess what?' he said. 'You know that new fridge at home? The Chilltastic RV? Frost Free. Triple Thermostat. Fast Freeze control. You know the one? The new one? Well, we made the whole kitchen collapse. Really. It's all broken to bits, the floor and everything. And, get this, the Chilltastic fell right down through the floor. Crash.'

Dad turned again. His eyes seemed to focus a little. He looked at Sam as if he thought they might have met somewhere. 'Fridge,' he said, like he was pushing the word out against some kind of pressure.

'Yes, yes,' said Sam. 'We broke the fridge. The new Chilltastic. It's all bashed and dented and it's probably broken for good.'

Dad took a couple of faltering steps towards him.

Sam held his breath. *It's working*, he thought. Behind Dad, he saw the hatching alien poke yet another leg out of the cocoon, then slowly pull its body out through the crack. It clung to the outside of the cocoon, swaying and turning its head from side to side. A glowing orange spider, the size of a large dog.

'Dad, Dad, quick!' Sam said. 'We need to get out of here. The alien is hatching, and then it's going to eat us all up. Quick!'

'Fridge,' said Dad, sounding a bit more like himself. He looked around. His gaze seemed more focussed, more familiar. He shook his head, vaguely.

'Dad! Help us!'

The alien was stretching its long legs, one by one. It made a chattering noise. Sam thought it looked hungry. He struggled desperately to move his arms.

'The aliens are hatching. They're going to eat us up if we don't get out of here.'

At that moment the baby alien launched itself off the cocoon. It shot across the cave and hovered for a second above Dad's head. Then it swooped down and landed on Sam with a thump. Sam yelled. Dad stepped towards him and then stood undecided.

'Dad!' yelled Sam.

'Mr Miller. Help!' yelled Max.

Dad stepped closer and stopped again. He lifted his arms, hands opening and shutting. He said, 'Fridge.'

Then he seemed to make up his mind and he lurched decisively towards the alien.

Suddenly there were running footsteps and Dad was shoved aside. It was Professor Vlastov.

'Do not disturb it,' he said. 'It must feed.'

He fumbled at his pocket trying to get the phone. Dad leaped at the professor, grabbed him around the middle, and they both fell to the floor with a crash. They rolled around, the professor still trying to reach his phone, Dad trying to pin the professor's arms and hold him down.

Sam struggled and squirmed with the glowing, chattering baby alien clinging to his chest. It was quite heavy.

It lowered its head.

'Sam!' Max cried. 'Oh no!'

Struggling as hard as he could, and yelling, 'Get off! Get off!' Sam glanced at Dad. Professor Vlastov had got his phone out. The red light was glowing brightly and he pressed a button and spoke into it.

Dad looked confused. He let go of the professor and stepped away, arms hanging limply, and shook his head. Then suddenly he twitched and leaped at the professor and grabbed him around the neck. They teetered together across the cave and bashed into the wall.

Sam looked back up at the alien. It was extending a thin tube, like a drinking straw, towards his face. Maybe it was planning to suck out his brains like a milkshake. It made a rasping noise, as if it was clearing its throat. From the end of the tube a gleaming blob of thick liquid formed, smoking and hissing slightly. The blob swelled and grew. Sam watched almost mesmerised. Was the hungry alien drooling?

The blob of mucus swelled and began to drip slowly, like syrup from a spoon. Steph was making desperate, muffled, grunting noises.

Her eyes were rolling around in a significant way.

All at once Sam remembered her disgusting story about how flies vomit on their food to dissolve it. Sam shrank back from the descending blob of hissing smoking drool. It was some kind of acid and it was going to dissolve his face.

He struggled, panic-stricken. He tried to jerk the alien off him, but it hung on tightly with the horny pincers on the end of each of its legs. Sam tried to turn his head away. He twisted his neck as far as he could. The smoking mucus was almost touching his cheek. He screwed up his face and shut his eyes.

The air started to burn.

Chapter Eighteen

As he lay there helplessly, waiting for the chattering baby alien to dissolve his face, Sam had one last, desperate idea. Summoning all his strength, he flung himself sideways. The alien hung on, but the blob of mucus swung like a pendulum that stretched and struck Sam's shoulder with a splat and a hiss. The alien shrieked and jerked its head from side to side. Strings of mucus flew around. Max yelped.

Sam felt a sharp burning pain in his shoulder. Some of the sticky threads that bound it started to loosen and dissolve. He struggled to free his arm. More threads parted where the bits of smoking mucus had landed.

With an enormous effort, he finally yanked his arm free. It felt weak and strange and his shoulder was burning, but he pulled it back and punched the alien. The alien gave a high-pitched screech and shot into the air.

'Go, Sam!' yelled Max.

Sam tore at the threads around his chest with his free arm. He pulled his other arm out and shoved and ripped, trying to get his legs free. It was like getting out of a very tight sticky sleeping bag.

On the far side of the cave Dad and Professor Vlastov were still on the floor. The professor managed to get his phone to his mouth again, pressed a button and said, 'Stop this! Stop this!'

Dad hesitated. He looked at Professor Vlastov, and then he looked across at Sam. He didn't seem to know what to do. He wasn't exactly hypnotised, but he wasn't back to normal yet, either. He seemed to be stuck somewhere in between.

His lips moved. 'Fridge,' he said uncertainly.

The professor pressed another button and said, 'Help me. Now.'

Uncle Andy came running into the cave. He flung himself on Dad and knocked him flat.

'Sam!' Max yelled.

Sam looked around. The baby alien was sitting on the fat sticky bundle that was Steph. Another blob of mucus was already forming and dripping towards Steph's face. She stared helplessly up at it. Her eyes were terrified. Sam flung himself across Max and thumped into the alien. It screeched again and flew away.

He clambered off Max and Steph, tore the last of the threads away from his legs and staggered to his feet.

'There's no time to unwrap you now,' he gasped. 'I'll just roll you.'

Sam started with Em, who was closest to the door. He heaved and rolled and dragged her down the tunnel and out the door into the storeroom. Then he turned and saw the alien hovering above Steph. He lunged at it, flapping his arms. It darted away.

Then Sam dragged and rolled Steph along the tunnel and went back for Max.

Suddenly Professor Vlastov grabbed Sam from behind, clamping his arms painfully behind his back. Sam struggled and yelled and kicked but it made no difference.

The professor's voice was soft and calm. 'Stop there. This ends now. No more. The alien must feed.'

Dad was still on the floor, gasping for breath and clutching his head. He didn't look good. Uncle Andy was standing over him.

Sam fought, but Professor Vlastov was strong. He half pulled, half carried Sam into the middle of the cave where the alien was hovering like an enormous wasp. Its blob of mucus vibrated and smoked. Behind it a second baby was already emerging from a cocoon, three spindly legs waving in the air.

'No, no!' Sam yelled, twisting away, trying to kick the professor's legs.

Suddenly there was an anxious, whining bark. Everyone turned to see Moriarty bounding ferociously into the cave trailing a bitten-through rope. With a tremendous snarl he leaped at Professor Vlastov.

The professor let go of Sam. Sam fell, got back to his feet and ran. He shoved Max towards the door, then ran back, thumped Uncle Andy, grabbed Dad by the arm, pulled him to his feet and gave him a push. Dad tottered towards the tunnel.

Moriarty was hanging onto Professor Vlastov's leg and growling like a lion. There was a clattering noise as the phone fell from the professor's hand and spun across the rocky floor. Sam dived full length and grabbed it.

It had at least twenty buttons.

Uncle Andy turned towards him. Sam jabbed a button on the phone. The red light glowed. 'Stop, stop!' he yelled into it. Uncle Andy kept coming. That wasn't right.

Sam pressed another couple of buttons. 'Stop,' he yelled, ducking under Uncle Andy's clutching hands and sprinting across the cave.

Uncle Andy turned and followed. Sam tried one more time, desperately jabbing at the phone. Uncle Andy kept coming.

Sam shook the phone. He threw it onto the floor and jumped on it with both feet.

There was a satisfying crunch. The red light blinked off. Uncle Andy stopped dead. His hands flopped at his sides. Sam grabbed his arm, yanked him across the cave and pushed him into the tunnel. Then he ran back, dragged Moriarty away from the professor and pulled him towards the door.

Everything seemed to be happening at once. Max was yelling, Em and Steph were groaning. Moriarty was growling, the alien was screeching and Dad was shouting something. Uncle Andy staggered and fell over Max, who was wedged in the doorway. Then Professor Vlastov rushed into the tunnel and tried to drag Max back into the cave.

The alien swooped down along the tunnel. Everyone lurched back. Max still blocked the doorway, so Sam shoved him into the storeroom. He grabbed Moriarty's collar and pulled him through the door. The alien hovered, dived at Sam and grabbed him around the face and chest, its eight legs clamping like metal pincers. It lowered its head, the blob of mucus smoking and hissing.

Suddenly the alien was yanked away. Dad heaved it aside and shoved Sam into the store-room. The alien screeched and chattered, then dashed at Dad's face. He thrust it back and slammed the door shut with an enormous clang.

There was a screeching, chattering, thumping racket on the far side of the door, and then there was silence.

Sam slumped, limp and gasping, against the pile of rocks. He was aching and bruised, and he hurt all over. His shoulder stung where the alien had burnt it. Moriarty licked his face anxiously. Sam patted Moriarty's hairy head. 'Good dog,' he said.

After a moment he began to take in what was happening around him. Dad and Uncle Andy still looked dazed, blinking and muttering to them-selves. A couple of confused-looking Magic Mart teenagers were coming uncertainly down the stairs.

'Hey, Sam!' Max called out. 'That was amazing. But don't just sit there. Unwrap us. It's really awful in here.'

Sam groaned. He couldn't be bothered to get to his feet so he half crawled, half dragged himself to where the others lay. He unwrapped Em and Steph's mouths first, so they could talk and breathe more easily. They spluttered and coughed and spat.

'That was horrible,' said Em. 'I thought we were going to die. I thought it was going to eat us. That was *really* horrible.'

'I know,' said Steph. 'I thought it was going to dissolve me and suck me up, just like that.'

'And when it flew in. I mean, it was so huge, wasn't it? And I bet my costume is completely ruined.'

'It's like the mosquitoes,' said Steph. 'You know, they live in the air, but their babies hatch in the water. And that thing, it lives in space, but it has its babies on earth. That's really interesting, isn't it?'

Sam couldn't help snorting as he unwrapped Max's head. It sounded like his sisters were recovering already.

'What will the babies eat now, though?' Steph asked. 'We'll have to give them something. Poor things. They'll need a good meal before they can fly away.'

'Don't be stupid,' said Sam. 'You can't be sorry for them. They were going to eat us up.'

'Astro-entomology,' Steph said thoughtfully. 'That's what the professor said. That's the study of space insects, I guess.'

'Where is the professor?' Sam asked. He looked

around the storeroom. Dad and Uncle Andy were wandering about vaguely, but there was no sign of Professor Vlastov. Had he gone upstairs?

Sam suddenly felt sick. In all the confusion, had the professor got out of the cave?

Sam went across to the door and turned the handle.

'Careful, Sam,' called Em.

He pulled it open a couple of centimetres, put his eye to the gap and peered in.

At first all he saw was the forest of dangling cocoons. The cave was completely silent. He pulled the door wider and stepped through. When nothing stirred, he went along the tunnel into the cave. There was no sign of the baby aliens, and there was no sign of the professor, either.

Most of the remaining cocoons were still glowing green, but a few were turning slightly orange. Two were empty. Two babies had hatched and gone.

As he tip-toed across the cave, Sam stepped on something soft. He looked down, then bent and picked up Professor Vlastov's black furry hat.

On the floor there was a wet mark, a couple of buttons, a shoelace, and a black leather glove. That was all.

The professor had been dissolved and the baby aliens had eaten their first meal, and flown away into space.

Sam stumbled back into the Magic Mart basement and shut the door behind him.

It was all over.

When Max and Em and Steph were unwrapped, they all climbed back up the stairs. Dad and Uncle Andy followed as if they were in a dream. Moriarty was the only one with any energy at all. He barked and whined and wagged his tail.

Max rang his mum from Uncle Andy's office. Sam could hear her yelling in relief down the phone. Uncle Andy opened the filing cabinet, pulled out a bottle and a couple of mugs and poured a drink for himself and Dad. They both sank into the office chairs and closed their eyes.

Sam flopped down on the floor just inside the door. Steph was still talking about the baby aliens. 'We'll have to arrange to feed them somehow,' she said. 'We could put a window in the door so we can see when they're hatching. And we can put food in there for them. I wonder what they eat.'

'People,' snapped Em. 'They eat people. They nearly ate *us*.'

Half listening to his sisters argue, Sam suddenly noticed he was sitting next to a small black suitcase. It was the one Professor Vlastov had been carrying the first time Sam saw him. From inside there came a faint snapping sound. With an eye on Dad and Uncle Andy, Sam reached out and nudged the suitcase out through the office doorway. The others were too tired to notice.

He'd pick it up on the way out. After all, he'd built the robot himself. It wasn't stealing. The robot was his.

EpiLogue

Nearly two weeks had passed. The school holidays were almost finished and it was the day of the dancing concert.

Sam sat with the rest of his family in the school hall, waiting for Em's dance. Sam wished he could have worn his silver alien helmet for the concert. He'd have preferred to watch it like that, but Mum had said no. The hall was packed. There'd been hours and hours of dancing. Dozens of girls in different coloured costumes, dressed as flowers and as fairies, had danced in circles and in rows. They had gone on and on and on, but the end of the concert was still ages away.

Moriarty had stopped singing, and now he was sleeping under Sam's feet. Sam had fallen into a kind of trance, mesmerised by the never-ending dancing, and thinking over all the things that had happened since Professor Vlastov was dissolved by aliens in the basement of Magic Mart. It was awful that he'd been eaten, but the professor had fed lots of people to the aliens, and if his plan had succeeded, Sam, Em, Steph and Max would have all been dissolved and eaten up too. And maybe Dad and Uncle Andy and the Magic Mart teenagers, as well.

Steph sat next to Sam, sniffing. Anyone would think she was crying because of the awful concert, but Sam knew she was sad because the last of the baby aliens had finally hatched and flown away. Steph had been feeding the babies with buckets of MØLK and banana custard. Apparently they didn't need to eat fresh meat. In fact, they seemed to eat just about anything. Steph had named all the babies, and this morning the youngest one, Starlight, had finally left the nest.

The mother alien had visited the cocoons many times while they were hatching. She'd once made a terrible mess trying to wrap up a bucket of banana custard in sticky threads. After that, Steph had left out some watermelons, and the alien wrapped them up neatly and stacked them in a corner of the cave.

Although most people didn't know it, Starlight's flight from the nest would be the last mysterious light to be seen in the sky above Magic Mart.

Max sat on Sam's other side. It was strange that someone would come to a dancing concert when they didn't have to. But something funny was going on with Max. Em's brave 'Sparkle, sparkle' dance in the cave seemed to have affected his brain. Max had sidled up to Sam one day at Magic Mart and said in a very casual kind of way, 'Umm. Can you get me a ticket for your sister's concert?'

Sam was so surprised that he spilled a bucketful of MØLK and banana custard he'd been preparing. 'What?' he gasped. 'Why?'

Max blushed. Then he mumbled, 'Your sister's amazing.'

Sam stared at Max with his mouth hanging open. 'Okay. I guess. If you want,' he finally said.

Max came often to visit, and whenever Em walked into the room he stared at her and blushed. Sam hoped this behaviour would wear off soon because it was very annoying.

Dad had taken the day off work to come to Em's concert. In fact he'd been taking a lot more time off recently. He and Uncle Andy were almost back to normal. It took a couple of days for the hypnotism to wear off completely, and Uncle Andy, who'd been under Professor Vlastov's control for much longer than Dad, still had dazed moments when he'd stare blankly into space for a minute or two. Every now and then he would suddenly say, 'There is nothing in the basement,' and then look surprised.

Uncle Andy put a Product Recall notice in the local paper, and people who had bought Bisky Bricks returned them to Magic Mart. Dad helped Uncle Andy collect the spare robot parts and half-built robots from all over town. They made a huge bonfire in the vacant lot behind Magic Mart and burnt them up. The smoke had risen blackly and smelled faintly fishy.

Apparently, Sam and Max were the only ones to build complete robots. No one else had managed to collect enough Bisky Bricks boxes to get all the parts. But lots of kids had half-built robots, and lots of houses in town were now needing minor repairs. Sam and Max had watched the bonfire mournfully. All those lovely robot parts, all gone.

Mum sat at the end of the row with Molly on her lap. Molly was wriggling around and shouting.

One good thing about nearly being eaten up by aliens was that Mum was so happy they were alive, she wasn't quite so furious about the kitchen. She was still fairly angry, though. And they weren't getting pocket money anytime soon.

The kitchen wasn't fixed yet, so they ate fish and chips a lot. Before the concert that afternoon, they'd had a barbecue with sausages, and a cake from the shop.

Moriarty lay under Sam's feet. He wanted to come with them wherever they went, and no one in the family had the heart to say no to him. So they sneaked him into the concert hall between them. Hardly ever in his life had Moriarty done the right thing at the right time, but when it had mattered, he'd bounded in like a ferocious tiger and saved everyone. Even Em was being nice to him. Now he was asleep, full of sausages and cake, and making rumbling noises with his stomach. Sam patted Moriarty's head with his foot.

At last the curtain came up for Em's dance. They all straightened in their seats as the music started playing the 'Sparkle, sparkle' song, and Em and Bethany pranced onto the stage. Em's costume was incandescent. People in the front row gasped and put their hands over their eyes. Em hadn't managed to unpick all the alien's sticky threads from the costume, so she'd just covered the whole thing with glitter. With the twinkling lights and the sequins and mirrors, it was truly amazing.

Bethany kept wincing and turning her head away from Em's dazzling costume. When Em did the dramatic jumping step Bethany flinched, stumbled over her own feet, staggered to the side of the stage and fell out of sight into the wings.

Em carried on dancing. She was finally doing

the solo she'd always wanted. Max sang along, clapping his hands. Sam was shocked to find that he, too, was humming the tune.

'*Sparkle, sparkle, just the same*
As the sun's most sparkly rays.
Sparkle, sparkle, like a flame,
Glint and glisten, flash and blaze.'

After Em's dance there was enormous applause. Happiness welled up inside Sam. He felt really good. There was a lot to be happy about, after all. Firstly, no one in the family had been dissolved and eaten up by aliens. Secondly, even a truly awful dancing concert must end sometime.

And finally, there was a beautiful silver robot hidden behind his shoes on the floor of his bedroom cupboard. Max had his, too. They'd both been in the professor's black suitcase. Sam had successfully smuggled the snapping, humming suitcase out of Magic Mart while Dad and Uncle Andy were too dazed and confused to notice.

Sam's robot was very frisky. It wanted to play all the time. Moriarty still didn't like it, and he growled whenever he saw it. But it wasn't as aggressive as before. It behaved more or less like a silver metallic puppy—just as if the professor had never modified it to hypnotise people and lead them to an alien nest to be dissolved and eaten.

The robot could cartwheel around the room

and flip itself onto the top of the bookshelf. Its eyes didn't glow a bright angry red, although occasionally they gave a faint flicker. True, it had once ripped a pillow to bits, covering the bedroom with shreds of foam but, really, it had only been playing.

Sam felt his mouth smiling all by itself. He couldn't be happier. The applause for Em's dance went on for ages. She sparkled and smiled and bowed.

And Sam clapped until his hands stung.

About The author

Judith Rossell's first novel was *Jack Jones and the Pirate Curse*, a riotous piratical adventure full of swashbuckling thrills. *Sam and the Killer Robot* is her second. Judith is best known for *I Spy with Inspector Stilton* and *Inspector Stilton and the Missing Jewels*, the sumptuously illustrated puzzle books starring the ingenious rat detective, Inspector Stilton. Her other puzzle titles include *The Lost Treasure of the Green Iguana*, *The Haunted Castle of Count Viper* and *The Mystery of the Golden Crocodile*, and she has illustrated books by other writers, including the Children's Book Council of Australia's 1999 shortlisted title, *How to Guzzle Your Garden* (by Jackie French), and the popular *Blackbread the Pirate* (by Garth Nix). Judith lives in Melbourne, Australia.

SAM AND THE
KILLER ROBOT